"How do you expect a man to react when you look like a candidate in a wet T-shirt contest?" Benedict said.

Startled, Riley glanced down at her sodden shirt. Raising her eyes again, she blurted, "But you're not—I mean, you're my employer! I'm your housekeeper!"

"I also happen to be a man," he pointed out, a disconcerting glint in his eyes.

Riley had known from the start that she'd have to rein in her attraction to Benedict Falkner. But he'd clearly indicated that he saw her as domestic help, nothing else.

Mutual lust, however, was totally different. Thrilling, surprising…and potentially disastrous.

It was only his male hormones reacting, she told herself. It didn't mean he intended to carry things any further, to compromise their employer-employee relationship….

Did it?

Dear Reader,

Summer is over and it's time to kick back into high gear. Just be sure to treat yourself with a luxuriant read or two (or, hey, all six) from Silhouette Romance. Remember—work hard, play harder!

Although October is officially Breast Cancer Awareness month, we'd like to invite you to start thinking about it now. In a wonderful, uplifting story, a rancher reluctantly agrees to model for a charity calendar to earn money for cancer research. At the back of that book, we've also included a guide for self-exams. Don't miss Cara Colter's must-read *9 Out of 10 Women Can't Be Wrong* (#1615).

Indulge yourself with megapopular author Karen Rose Smith and her CROWN AND GLORY series installment, *Searching for Her Prince* (#1612). A missing heir puts love on the line when he hides his identity from the woman assigned to track him down. The royal, brooding hero in Sandra Paul's stormy *Caught by Surprise* (#1614), the latest in the A TALE OF THE SEA adventure, also has secrets—and intends to make his beautiful captor pay…by making her his wife!

Jesse Colton is a special agent forced to play pretend boyfriend to uncover dangerous truths in the fourth of THE COLTONS: COMANCHE BLOOD spinoff, *The Raven's Assignment* (#1613), by bestselling author Kasey Michaels. And in Cathie Linz's MEN OF HONOR title, *Married to a Marine* (#1616), combat-hardened Justice Wilder had shut himself away from the world—until his ex-wife's younger sister comes knocking…. Finally, in Laurey Bright's tender and true *Life with Riley* (#1617), free-spirited Riley Morrisset may not be the perfect society wife, but she's exactly what her stiff-collared boss needs!

Happy reading—and please keep in touch.

Mary-Theresa Hussey

Mary-Theresa Hussey
Senior Editor

Please address questions and book requests to:
Silhouette Reader Service
U.S.: 3010 Walden Ave., P.O. Box 1325, Buffalo, NY 14269
Canadian: P.O. Box 609, Fort Erie, Ont. L2A 5X3

Life with Riley

LAUREY BRIGHT

SILHOUETTE *Romance*

Published by Silhouette Books

America's Publisher of Contemporary Romance

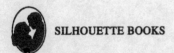

SILHOUETTE BOOKS

ISBN 0-373-19617-2

LIFE WITH RILEY

Copyright © 2002 by Daphne Clair de Jong

Visit Silhouette at www.eHarlequin.com

Printed in U.S.A.

Books by Laurey Bright

Silhouette Romance

Tears of Morning #107
Sweet Vengeance #125
Long Way from Home #356
The Rainbow Way #525
Jacinth #568
The Mother of His Child #918
Marrying Marcus #1558
The Heiress Bride #1578
Life with Riley #1617

Silhouette Special Edition

Deep Waters #62
When Morning Comes #143
Fetters of the Past #213
A Sudden Sunlight #516
Games of Chance #564
A Guilty Passion #586
The Older Man #761
The Kindness of Strangers #820
An Interrupted Marriage #916

Silhouette Intimate Moments

Summers Past #470
A Perfect Marriage #621

LAUREY BRIGHT

has held a number of different jobs, but has never wanted to be anything but a writer. She lives in New Zealand, where she creates the stories of contemporary people in love that have won her a following all over the world. Visit her at her Web site, http://www.laureybright.com.

Chapter One

"*Damn!*" Too late, Riley Morrisset slammed on the brake.

Backing out of the narrow shopping-mall parking space, she'd turned the wheel too early. The ominous metallic shriek of her front bumper scraping against the side of the car next to hers had come all too clearly through her open window.

Groaning, she shoved strands of straight brown hair from her eyes, pulled on the brake and switched off the key before pushing open her door and going to inspect the damage.

Her ancient red Corona seemed unmarked, but the gleaming dark-blue BMW showed a long, telltale gouge right down to the metal, with a nasty dent at the end.

"Damn, damn, damn!" She'd have to leave her name and address for the owner. But first she'd better shift the Corona from the path of other traffic. Already a battered gray van was entering the end of the lane.

Quickly she returned to her car, switching the engine on.

The van was nosing into a space farther up the row, but there could be other cars entering soon. Riley grasped the gear lever, then jumped as a dark-sleeved arm reached in the open window and long male fingers switched off the key. At the same time a grim masculine voice said, "Oh, no, you don't!"

Riley's strangled yelp of alarm was drowned by her horn as she pressed the flattened palm of her free hand down on it.

The sound was abruptly cut off when strong fingers gripped her wrist and forcibly lifted her hand away. "What the hell—" the man said.

Looking up in panic, Riley had a confused impression of blazing eyes—a startling meld of navy blue and deep, deep gray—close-drawn black brows and a threatening expression, before she realized that his other hand had removed the ignition key with its attendant house keys and large plastic Snoopy tag.

She snatched at Snoopy, but didn't get a good grip, and the keys jangled to the floor of the car.

Riley tried to close the window with her free hand, but the manual winder was stuck again. Under her breath she cursed the garage mechanic who was supposed to have fixed it.

Twisting in her seat, she fumbled with her free hand for the knob to lock the door. Finding that her face was within an inch of the implacable hand encircling her wrist, she sank her teeth into the man's flesh, tasting soap and warm, slightly salty male skin.

He let fly a vicious word and pulled back but didn't

release her. Desperately Riley opened her mouth wide and screamed. A loud, aggressive, attention-getting scream.

The mugger muttered something savage and dropped her wrist at last as pounding footsteps made him look away from her.

Riley was hugely relieved to see two large men bearing down on them. Both wore torn jeans and studded belts, and their muscular arms were heavily tattooed. One would have been described as Caucasian by the police. He looked as though he might be on intimate terms with them. His big pale head was shaved bald, and the orange T-shirt stretched over his chest had a foam-fanged, spike-collared bulldog printed on the front. The other man was Maori. Well-greased dreadlocks fell to massive brown shoulders bared by a black bushman's vest.

Riley expected her attacker to flee. Instead he stood his ground as the unlikely Galahads bore down on him. Riley tried the window winder again without success, mentally vowing to boil the inept mechanic in his own sump oil.

"Trouble, lady?" the bald guy queried, casting a threatening look at the man beside her, who was half a head shorter. His companion moved so that they were hemming him in, glowering down at him.

Before Riley could say a thing the man answered, "She sure is. She damaged my car and was making a getaway. When I tried to stop her she bit me."

Riley's mouth fell open. She shifted a hunted brown gaze to the BMW, then back to him, her heart plunging like a stone on the end of a plumb line. For the first time she looked at him properly.

His suit might have come out of the pages of *GQ*.

And with it he wore a white shirt with a fine gray shadow stripe and a tie.

A tie. Probably silk, probably with a designer name hidden somewhere discreetly behind its elegant blue and maroon design. For all she knew, it was an old school tie proclaiming his presumed respectability.

Even his accent was cultured—with neither flat antipodean vowels nor a fruity fake-British affectation.

He didn't look like a mugger. Not a bit.

Oh, hell!

Her would-be rescuers looked from her to him, and the long-haired one ambled over to inspect the BMW. His lips pursed, and he sorrowfully shook his shining black dreadlocks. "Got a panel beater's job there, mate," he said sympathetically.

Riley turned her head to confront her attacker. "*Your* car?" she squeaked.

"My car," the not-a-mugger-after-all confirmed, his dark gaze still accusing as he looked down the arrogant slope of his nose.

She closed her eyes for a moment, then flicked them open. "Prove it," she said, daring to look him straight in the face—a smooth-shaven, stubborn-jawed face, with broad cheekbones and a wide forehead under impeccably groomed black hair that hinted at a firmly discouraged wave. He probably had quite a nice mouth when it wasn't set in an angry line, the lips well-defined and not unduly narrow.

For a long second he just stared back at her. Then he dug in his trouser pocket and took out a small leather folder, flicking a plastic tag from it and pressing a button with his thumb. "Don't let her take off," he said to the bald man.

"I wasn't going to!" Riley said indignantly as The

Suit walked away, pausing to read her number plate on his way toward the BMW. Memorizing it, she supposed.

Another car tooted gently behind hers and swung to go round it. Baldy moved to the front of the Corona and stood foursquare with his arms folded, facing Riley through the windscreen. A blue dragon writhed on his brawny forearm.

Great. Now he was *guarding* her for heaven's sake. She glared at him, every bit as belligerent as the bulldog on his shirt.

The other car nudged by with about two inches to spare. Riley wouldn't have even tried to negotiate that space.

Her watchdog was looking to the other side. She followed his gaze and saw that the BMW's driver door was open.

The man in the suit slammed it and came back to her window. "Satisfied? Now can we exchange insurance companies and addresses? I'll see that yours gets a bill for the damage."

The watchdog and his mate were looking at Riley almost as censoriously as the car's owner.

"Okay?" Dreadlocks queried her.

"Yes," Riley conceded reluctantly. "Thank you for coming over. I thought I was being assaulted." Dammit, she *had* been assaulted. "He grabbed me!" She transferred her fulminating gaze to the man between them.

"To stop you running away," he agreed without a blink. "*You're* not hurt, are you?" As he spoke he lifted his hand and inspected a row of deep teethmarks in the pad of flesh just below his thumb.

Riley's wrist still tingled from his hold, but she

could see no sign of the remembered strength of his fingers, not even a slight redness. "No," she admitted.

"I'm sure we can sort it out from here." He nodded affably to her two heroes. "Can't we?" he asked her pointedly. "Thanks, though," he added to the knights errant, making Riley's already simmering blood almost boil over.

"Good luck, bro." Bulldog-shirt grinned.

"Women drivers, eh?" Dreadlocks commented as they turned away. He rolled a look at Riley and laughed.

Riley gritted her teeth. "I was going to drive back into the parking space," she told the man still standing by her window, and added distinctly, "before I left you my name and address. We *are* in the way here."

In her rearview mirror she saw another car coming slowly toward them. "See?" she insisted as he looked up and behind her.

"Be my guest." He stepped away to allow her room, and she carefully reparked.

When she got out he was standing between their two cars with a pen in his right hand and a small notebook in his left. He scribbled something on a white business card and handed it to her.

Before she could read it he offered her the notebook, opened at a blank page, and the slim gold pen. "Name, address, insurance company," he said tersely. "Mine's all on the card."

She shoved it into the back pocket of her jeans, taking the pen and notebook.

Hemmed into the space between the cars with him, she could smell his expensive suiting, and a hint of soap or aftershave. Something sort of woodsy, with an undertone of spice. And an over-priced brand name, no doubt.

She lowered her head, pushing back the strands of hair escaping her carelessly fastened ponytail.

"I suppose you do have a license?" he said.

About to write down her insurance company's name, she looked up. "Of course I have!"

"You scarcely look old enough," he said skeptically. "Is the car yours or your parents'?"

"I'm twenty-four," she snapped. "And the car's mine!"

His dispassionate gaze swooped from her dead-straight, too-fine hair escaping in hanks from its ponytail, to her ancient trainers, on the way taking in the baggy bottle-green T-shirt that concealed small but quite decently shaped breasts, and the comfortable, wash-softened jeans.

When she'd dressed, the jeans had seemed perfectly respectable. Now she was acutely conscious of the fading, thinned fabric at the knees—and the tear, barely perceptible this morning, that had widened when she'd bent to pick up a child who'd taken a tumble at the day care center where she worked.

Still, that was no reason for this stranger to eye her with what she strongly suspected was scorn. Her head instinctively went up in defiance. It was about level with his chin, which meant that he was under six feet by some inches. But the breadth of his shoulders and an unmistakable air of assurance more than made up for the height he didn't have.

Riley was used to literally looking up to people, but not many of them made her feel this intimidated. He was too big, too damned close, and she had no way of escape. "Don't crowd me," she said fiercely as his eyes swept up again to hers.

He stepped back, doubling the space between them to a meter or so. "Are you paranoid or something?"

"I don't have to be paranoid to be wary of strange men. Especially men who go round abusing innocent women." She handed back the notebook and pen, unflinchingly standing her ground as he came closer again to take it.

"I don't." His gaze this time lingered rather thoughtfully on her as he pushed his hands into his pockets, sweeping back the sides of his jacket. "You're very small. I suppose you would feel—"

"You're not exactly Arnold Schwarzenegger yourself, are you?" Riley didn't like being reminded of her deficient height.

With deliberate insolence she returned the look he'd given her, contemptuously examining the solid chest behind the pristine shirting, the black leather belt fastened about a taut waist above lean hips and what looked like rather well-muscled thighs encased in trousers so nicely fitted they must have been tailor-made.

Reaching his polished leather shoes—Italian, at a guess—she brought her gaze back to his, glad that she didn't have to get a crick in her neck to do so. She wasn't actually keen on very tall men—they made her feel her own lack of inches too acutely.

Surprisingly, his mouth twitched, and a spark of laughter lit his eyes. "Do *you* want to look like Arnie?" he asked her.

"Of course I don't—"

"Neither do I," he cut in. "Luckily."

So he was quite happy as he was. Self-satisfied jerk.

He took his hands out of his pockets and looked down at the one she'd bitten.

"I'm sorry about that," Riley said uncomfortably. "How bad is it?" Instinctively, as she would have done with a hurt child at the day care center, she took his hand to inspect the wound.

His palm was broad, his fingers long and blunt-ended with clean, short-cut nails. An expanding strap held the stainless steel watch on his wrist. She'd have expected gold.

Again that subtle scent tantalized her. She turned his wrist and paused, momentarily fascinated by the tiny pulse beating under the skin. There was no blood although the marks of her teeth were hideously clear.

"You really thought I was attacking you," he said to the top of her head.

"Yes." Riley released him.

"I didn't mean to terrify you."

Riley's head jerked up. "I wasn't terrified. I was furious."

He grinned suddenly, a grin of pure amusement. She'd been right about his mouth—it was rather nice really. And his teeth were white and straight.

Capped, most likely. He looked the type who could afford it. She ran her tongue over her own slightly crooked left canine, a habit she'd had since childhood, making her lips involuntarily part.

"So was I," he said.

"I *was* going to stop and leave my name and number," she insisted. "You didn't have to jump on me like that."

"The way you raced back to your car, it looked as though you were making a fast getaway," he pointed out.

"If I was going to cut and run I wouldn't have stopped to check what I'd done," she argued. Her gaze going to the ugly scrape on his car, she muttered gloomily, "I don't suppose the repair bill will be less than the no claims discount on my policy." Not on a BMW. They'd probably have to import the paint from Europe or something.

"I could get it assessed and let you know the cost if you'd rather just pay for it."

"Mmm," she said doubtfully. "Well…"

"Is that a problem?"

Riley didn't suppose it would be any use trying to explain to him just how much of a problem it was. She would lay odds that he'd been born chewing on a mouthful of silver spoons—or if not, that he owned a drawerful of them now. She sighed. "I'll work it out. I'm responsible."

"I'm glad to hear it."

Her indignation resurfaced. "I *am* a responsible person. And a good driver!" Although she'd learned in America she'd become accustomed to driving on the "wrong" side of the road in England even before coming to live in New Zealand.

Silently he turned his head and looked at the damage she'd done.

"We all make mistakes!" she protested. "*You* did, when you thought I was taking off."

His considering, gunmetal eyes met her defiant brown ones. "Okay," he said slowly. "I accept that."

Riley's relief was disproportionate. She couldn't help breaking into a smile, her wide mouth tilting up at the corners, her lips parting. "Thank you," she said.

He must have noticed the crooked tooth, because his gaze remained riveted on her mouth and there was the strangest expression on his face, as if he'd just seen something that he found utterly disconcerting.

Maybe he was a dentist. After all, the tooth was a very small imperfection—one of many, including the few freckles peppering her nose—and surely not all that noticeable?

Involuntarily her tongue moved almost protectively to touch the tooth, but something rebelled against showing her self-consciousness and she quickly altered the movement, instead unthinkingly moistening her lips.

His head twitched up slightly, and his eyes narrowed as again they met hers.

No! she thought, blinking at the glint she saw in the metallic depths. Surely not…

Then it was gone, his expression bland and his eyes hooded as he stepped back again. She must have been mistaken.

He turned and walked around the back of his car, not looking at her again until he reached the door, then he studied her over the BMW's shiny, dustless roof. "Do you have a job?" he asked abruptly.

Riley blinked. "Part-time."

"Forget the insurance," he said. "I believe in people facing up to the consequences of their actions, but I'll have this fixed and maybe we can come to some arrangement."

Riley stiffened. "What kind of arrangement?" she asked suspiciously, wondering if she hadn't been mistaken after all. She shouldn't have licked her lips like that. Had he thought she was giving him a come-on?

He looked startled, then laughed as his gaze dropped disbelievingly to her baggy T-shirt and the damaged jeans before returning to her face. "Not that sort." His tone implied that the idea was too absurd to consider.

The skin over her cheekbones burned. So she'd been wrong. He wasn't in the least tempted by her unremarkable body, but he needn't rub it in.

"I was thinking along the lines of time payment," he told her.

Riley swallowed her unreasonable humiliation. "That's very considerate. I…I am sorry about your car. I hope you're not going to be too inconvenienced."

"It'll be a couple of days in the panel shop, I guess. I'll have to find some other way of getting into the office, that's all."

"Where do you live?"

"Kohi," he answered. "Why?"

Kohimarama, one of Auckland's more expensive suburbs, was twenty minutes or so from her shared flat in Sandringham. Perhaps thirty in the rush hour. "I could take you to work and drive you home afterward while your car's being fixed."

He looked at her tired little car, and she said quickly, "It's actually quite respectable when it's cleaned up, but I suppose you'd prefer not to be driven round in this. It was a dumb idea."

His expression said he was going to refuse again, but he paused. "What about your job?"

"I work from one till five. If you don't need to leave your office on the dot of five then it's not a problem. Just let me know when you want to be picked up and where.''

''All right,'' he said abruptly. ''I accept.''

Riley broke into another smile. ''Good!''

''I just hope you're right about being a good driver—usually. I'll phone you.'' He gave her a curt nod and climbed into his car.

Riley got into hers and waited until he'd left before backing out again, unwilling to run any risk of making another mistake in front of that man.

She didn't even know his name. His card was in her back pocket, but she'd scarcely glanced at it when he gave it to her.

After driving home more cautiously than usual, she drew into the lopsided double garage outside an old, much-repainted-and-renovated villa.

The driver's window closed without a hitch, and she muttered at it darkly before hauling grocery bags from the back seat, slamming the door with an elbow and then going up the worn back steps to tap on the door with her sneaker-clad toe.

Linnet Yeung opened the door to the big old-fashioned kitchen, her pretty, golden-skinned face breaking into a smile as she reached for one of the bags.

Riley smiled back. One reason she liked Lin so much was her helpful nature. Also she was the only one of Riley's friends who was shorter than she was.

As they unpacked the groceries, Lin said, ''Harry found a new girl so he won't be eating here tonight.'' She grinned and rolled her brown eyes. ''He does look tasty when he's all togged up.''

''Mmm,'' Riley agreed, taking out a packet of pasta from a bag. Harry was part Samoan, part Maori and part Irish, and the rest was anybody's guess—which made him a pure full-blooded Kiwi, he joked, New Zealand being such a racial melting pot. "Logie and Sam?" she inquired, placing the pasta on the counter.

"They wouldn't miss dinner when it's your turn to cook." Lin opened the fridge to stow some butter. "How was your day?"

Riley lifted a red string bag of onions. "I pranged someone's car at the shopping center."

"Ooh!" Lin winced in sympathy. "Was it bad?"

"A scratch, really, but it was a BMW. The owner was quite decent about it considering I'd just bitten him."

"You *what?*"

The explanation sent Lin into giggles as she folded the empty bags. "So what's his name?"

Riley fished in her pocket for the card she'd shoved in there. "Benedict Falkner," she read aloud, then squinted, trying the name against the face that came vividly to mind. She'd never have guessed Benedict. "I think he's a dentist." Consulting the card again, she corrected herself. "No, actually, this says Executive Director, Falkner Industries."

"And he drives a Beemer? He could probably afford to buy himself a whole new car—and he's making you pay for a teeny little scratch?"

"He believes in people taking responsibility for their mistakes."

Lin snorted down her delicate little nose. "Pompous git!"

Riley laughed. "A good-looking one."

"How old?"

"Um, thirtyish, probably."

Lin tipped her head to one side inquiringly, her sloe eyes dancing.

"He was big," Riley said. "Well...not tall for a man, but...he seems to need a lot of room."

And yet he hadn't allowed her much room, she recalled. Until she'd asked him not to crowd her and he'd stepped back.

"You fancied him, didn't you?" Lin teased.

"No chance," Riley retorted. But it wasn't really a denial. More a resigned acknowledgment that even if she had fancied Benedict Falkner, there was precious little hope of anything coming of it. He'd made his lack of sexual interest in her almost insultingly clear.

Besides, the man was out of her league, with his tailor-made suit and his expensive car and his business card embossed with the title Executive Director.

Chapter Two

The following evening Logie poked his long-faced, shaggy blond head around the door of the big lounge where Riley was watching television with Lin and Harry. "For you, Ri." He held out the portable receiver.

Riley jumped up from the floor where she'd been sitting with her back against the well-worn sofa and took the phone. "Hello?" She followed Logie's lanky form into the wide passageway, away from the sound of the TV, and he ambled back to the room he shared with his girlfriend, Samuela.

"Riley Morrisset?"

She'd have recognized the deep male voice anywhere. "Yes, Mr. Falkner."

Maybe she'd surprised him. It was a moment before he said, "My car's going to the panel beaters tomorrow. If you meant what you said, you could take me home from the office after work."

"Tell me where."

He gave her a midtown address and said, "Can you make it by five-thirty? There's a private car park under the building. My space is on the left, marked with my name."

Next day when she headed the car down the short, steep ramp, he was already waiting, holding a black briefcase.

Riley was fifteen minutes late.

She stopped the car and he opened the passenger door, climbed in and put the briefcase in front of him on the floor.

"Sorry," she said, "I got held up." One of the children at the day care center had mysteriously disappeared, and the entire staff and the little girl's parents had spent twenty anxious minutes searching before she was discovered, sulking under a pile of dress-up clothes in a large carton.

He didn't answer, pulling the seat belt across his chest and clipping it into the housing. Today the shirt with his dark suit was pale lavender and his tie a deep plum color.

She tried to tell herself it was dandified, but truthfully he looked terrific. And Riley hadn't changed out of her paint-stained yellow T-shirt and comfortable brown stretch leggings with a half-dried muddy patch on one knee.

"Do you know how to get to Kohi?" he asked, obviously uninterested in explanations.

"It's not my part of town, but I know where Kohimarama Road is."

"Head for that and I'll direct you from there."

He watched critically while she drove up the exit

ramp and eased the car into the flow of home-going commuters.

After three sets of traffic lights, he apparently decided that he wasn't going to have to grab the wheel from her or haul on the brake and leap for his life. Opening the briefcase, he said, "Do you mind if I work?"

"Feel free." She was only his driver, after all—temporarily.

He pulled out a laptop computer and opened it, then began tapping the keys. Next time they stopped for a red light she glanced at the screen, filled with some kind of graph. "Are you a workaholic?" she asked.

His fingers stilled momentarily. "I don't like to waste my time."

Riley's lips closed firmly, ostentatiously.

He looked at her and laughed. "And I had a feeling I was making you nervous."

"You were." The light changed, and she eased off the brake and moved the car forward.

"You drive quite well."

"I told you I do."

He didn't remind her that she'd driven less than well when she scratched his car. Riley supposed she ought to be grateful. "Don't let me disturb your work," she said crisply.

A car swerved into the lane ahead of them, and Riley braked. Her passenger said, "I guess you need to concentrate in this traffic, anyway."

They didn't speak again until he said, "Left at the next intersection." Within a few minutes he had directed her into a cul-de-sac of what looked like million-dollar, architect-designed homes. "Number thirty-five, down at the end."

"Wow!" The place was a symphony of curved cement-work painted a mellow, warm gold, with inset glass panels. Balconies, railed with elegant black wrought iron, had been cleverly tucked into the design, one with a spiral stairway to the ground. Some, Riley guessed, would have a distant sea view.

"You like it?"

Riley drew up outside. "It's fantastic!" Despite being architect-designed contemporary, the house woke vague memories of fairy-tale castles, perhaps because of its height and curved outlines. She turned to face him. "When shall I pick you up in the morning? I won't be late again."

"Eight-thirty?" As she nodded, his mouth curved in amusement and he lifted a hand to her cheek, rubbing at it gently with his thumb.

Before she could react, he'd drawn his hand away, looking at the smudge of green paint on his thumb. She saw he still had fading red marks at the base. Her cheeks stinging, she said, "How's your hand?"

"I'll live." He looked up at her. "Didn't it occur to you that it can be dangerous going around biting strangers? If you'd broken the skin you might have picked up something nasty."

The heat faded from her skin as her eyes widened. "Do you have anything nasty?"

"No!" His brows drew together. "No chance. I'm a regular blood donor."

"Well, you brought it up."

The frown cleared, but he looked a bit exasperated. "By the way," he said rather curtly, "I got an estimate on the damage to my car, and it probably wouldn't be worth your while claiming insurance. If it comes out to more I'll wear the difference."

That was a load off her mind. "Thank you, Mr. Falkner."

"Women who are on biting terms with me usually call me Benedict."

The tiniest glimmer in his eyes confirmed that he was teasing. Riley breathed in quickly. "Not Ben?"

"Only those who know me...intimately." His voice had deepened.

She didn't suppose he was short of women who'd at least like to know him intimately. "Are you married?" she asked him.

"No."

He'd think she was fishing. Was that wariness that she saw in his face now? Hastily she said, "Well, I'll see you in the morning. I really have to get home now."

Taking the hint, he opened the door, closing it behind him before he bent to say, "Thanks."

Riley turned the key and did a fast turn out of the cul-de-sac. At the first traffic light she tilted the rearview mirror and peered into it. A faint smudge of green still marked her cheekbone. Scrubbing at it with the heel of her hand, she blew a fine strand of hair away from her mouth.

No wonder Benedict Falkner had found her amusing. Maybe she should have her hair cut short. But it would need to be properly styled and then regularly maintained to look halfway decent, and hairdressers were expensive. She wore it just past shoulder length so she could keep it trimmed herself and tie it back out of the way.

Back at the house Samuela, swathed in a brightly colored sarong that left her smooth brown shoulders and plump arms bare, had her hands buried in a large bowl, and had hardly raised her tightly ringleted black head to say hello to Riley before ordering Logie to bring those carrots over if he'd finished murdering them. There was a strong smell of curry in the air. Tonight's dinner would be a triumph or a disaster. Sam's cooking knew no half measures.

Retreating to her room, Riley retrieved from the floor the satin pajamas her parents had sent her at Christmas, pulled the imitation-patchwork duvet over the bed and closed the book she'd dropped on the rag mat last night, placing it on the painted box that served as a night table.

She'd rushed out early to get the morning paper and study the Situations Vacant before going to her polytech course.

Closing the gaping door of her second-hand rimu wardrobe, she caught sight of herself in the full-length mirror and grimaced.

Impatiently she stripped off the grubby T-shirt and leggings and bundled them into an Ali Baba basket in the corner. At least in briefs and a bra she didn't look half grown. Her figure might be small but it was quite curvy.

Still, she couldn't go round wearing undies. She dragged a clean pair of shorts and another T-shirt from a drawer, put them on and went to the bathroom next to her room to wash her face.

The curry was one of Samuela's disasters. She kept apologizing as the others, red-eyed and spluttering, bravely mixed it with rice and washed it down with cold water. All night there was a constant parade to the bathroom, and the old pipes gurgled and thundered after each visit, keeping Riley half-awake until dawn.

When her alarm went off she huddled under the duvet in denial for ten minutes, but finally crawled out of bed, had a cool shower in an effort to wake herself properly, then made herself toast and coffee.

Back in her bedroom, she pulled out the dark-green skirt she wore for job interviews, and a short-sleeved, pin-tucked cream blouse she'd bought for a song in Singapore, buttoning it as she slid bare feet into heeled shoes that gave her a little extra height but were still comfortable to wear.

After dragging a brush over her hair, she picked up a hair tie and raced out to her car, slipping the elastic temporarily over her wrist.

The traffic was heavy at this time of the morning, and while waiting in a line of cars to move through a set of lights, Riley pulled back her hair and twisted the elastic band about it.

She drew up outside Benedict Falkner's house with ten minutes to spare and anxiously checked her appearance in the rearview mirror.

Her skin was even paler than normal, the freckles on her nose standing out against her skin. With her hair smoothed back her face seemed thin, the faint blue hollows under her eyes a legacy of her sleepless night.

On impulse she pulled the elastic tie off and tucked her hair back behind her ears.

She was surveying herself critically again when the passenger door opened and Benedict said, "Have I kept you waiting?"

Riley returned the mirror to its proper position. "I was early."

He climbed in, put a newspaper on the dashboard and parked a briefcase in front of his feet, giving Riley an appraising glance as he fastened his seat belt. "Going somewhere special?" he asked, eyeing the neat skirt and blouse.

Riley put the car into gear. "Maybe a job interview."

"What are you looking for?"

"Anything, really." If she didn't find a second job soon she'd have to give up her car. But without a car she couldn't make it to the day care center in time after leaving her class, meaning she'd have no job at all and no money. "Something with flexible hours that pays well, if I had a choice."

"You're some kind of artist, aren't you? I suppose it doesn't pay much."

Riley turned to look at him for a moment. "Artist?"

"Yesterday you were covered in paint. I thought..."

She laughed. "The artist is three years old. He wasn't too sure exactly what it was he was supposed to be painting—me, himself, or the paper I'd given him to do his picture on."

She slowed at the intersection to look for oncoming traffic, swung out of the cul-de-sac and changed gear again. Benedict was gazing through the windscreen at the oncoming traffic but probably thinking of something else.

"Are you married?" he asked her as she accelerated.

Riley threw him a startled look before returning her eyes to the road. "No." She'd asked him the same thing yesterday, she recalled.

A car shot out of a driveway ahead of them, and she flattened the brake. Benedict was jerked against his seat belt, the newspaper falling from the dashboard.

"Sorry," Riley gasped as the engine stalled.

"Not your fault. Bloody idiot," he added as the other car roared off ahead of them.

"Yes," Riley agreed. "There are lots of them around." Restarting the engine, she added, "And please don't say anything about pots calling kettles black."

"Wasn't even thinking of it," Benedict assured her blandly. He bent to pick up the newspaper, looking at the headlines. "So…what's the three-year-old artist's name?"

She thought he'd forgotten all about that remark. "Tamati. He's quite a sweetie." Her lips curved affectionately. "Bit of a mischief if you don't keep him occupied, though."

From the corner of her eye she saw his swift glance at her. "Tamati…Maori?"

"Mmm, his father's Maori." She slowed at a corner, peering carefully for other traffic before accelerating again.

"Uh-huh." Benedict unfolded the paper so he could read the front page. Later he turned to other pages, careful to fold them out of her way. By the time they reached his office building he'd read the main news and was perusing the business section.

When he made to fold it and gather up the rest, she said, "Do you want the Situations Vacant pages?"

"No. Do you?"

"If you can spare them, thanks."

"Have the lot, I've finished with it." He placed it on the dashboard again.

"Thanks. I'll be here at five-thirty," she promised. "Okay?"

"Look, you don't really need—"

"I feel bad about your car, and it's the least I can do, especially since you're willing to take your money in installments."

"All right," Benedict said at last, but his voice sounded clipped and distant. "If you insist."

When she fetched him, he nodded to her as he got in, not commenting on the fact that she was back in jeans and a T-shirt. She had made sure her face was clean and retied her hair but, anxious not to be late again, hadn't taken the time to change out of her work clothes. Benedict Falkner had already seen how she looked at the end of an afternoon helping to keep twenty children stimulated and happy. And anyway, she wasn't trying to impress him, was she?

As she merged the Corona into a stream of traffic, he reached for his briefcase, then apparently changed his mind, sitting back and folding his arms.

"If you want to work," she said, "it's okay."

For a moment she thought he hadn't heard her. "Right. I should."

He opened the briefcase and hauled out a folder filled with papers, flipping through it and making notes on the pages with a pencil.

"What do you actually do?" she asked after a while, unable to stem her curiosity completely. "I mean, what does your firm do?"

"Telecommunications and electronics, mainly," he answered, not looking up from the papers on his knee.

"We import parts, and design and build custom-made systems."

"Computers?"

"Industrial computers and communication systems. Not personal computers." He made another note on the page before him.

"And you're the executive director. Impressive."

He gave a crack of laughter. "When you own the company you can give yourself any impressive title you like."

Riley slowed for an intersection, then accelerated smoothly. "Is it a family business?"

He looked a little grim for a second. "You could say that—except I'm the only family I have."

"Did you inherit it?"

"No. I started from scratch."

He must have had a family once. Maybe he'd inherited capital. But maybe not. Despite the civilized suits and the expensive car and house, there was an edge to him, a toughness that showed through now and then and that she suspected he hadn't got from a cushioned life and a cultured education. "So how did you get to where you are today?"

He laughed again. "Hard work, low cunning and a certain amount of luck. But mainly it's a matter of setting goals and remaining focused. I knew what I wanted and how to get it, and didn't allow myself to be distracted by side issues."

Or let anything stand in his way, she guessed, a little chilled. "What did you want?"

"To be a millionaire before I was thirty," he said calmly.

He couldn't be much more than that now. He must have been driven, and she wondered where such sin-

gle-minded, naked ambition came from. "When did
you decide that?"

"I was eighteen."

Riley shook her head in wonder. "When I was
eighteen I had no idea what I wanted." Except her
independence from a loving but sometimes annoy-
ingly protective family who had spent years trying to
instill caution into her impulsive spirit. Eager to try
her wings, see the world and pay her own way, she'd
been restless, never settling, not knowing what she
was searching for until she landed in New Zealand
and knew she'd found her natural home. Or rather,
rediscovered it.

"What about now?" Benedict asked.

"I'm studying to teach English as a second language." She had finally settled on a career path that
excited her and promised a sense of purpose and use-
fulness, and the stimulation of interacting with people
from many cultures.

"You didn't say you were a student when I asked
if you had a job."

"You didn't ask." He'd seemed more interested in
whether she was earning enough to repay him for the
damage to his car.

"You must have a busy life. Study and part-time
work, as well as—"

He was interrupted by a low burring sound close
by that made Riley jump.

Benedict pulled a cell phone from his briefcase.
"Falkner here," he said into the receiver.

Riley tried not to listen, but she could hear an excited voice on the other end and Benedict's replies.
"Good God! When?... Where is she?... Tell her she's
not to think of that, and if you need anything... Give

me your number, I'll be in touch." He scribbled on the margin of the paper he'd been reading. "And your address? Thank you for contacting me."

Frowning, he pressed a button on the phone before putting it away.

"Trouble?" Riley asked.

"My housekeeper's had an accident. That was her daughter."

"Is she badly hurt?" Riley asked in concern.

"Cut her head on a piece of furniture. She's been stitched up, but they suspect she may have had a small stroke and that's why she fell."

"Oh, poor thing. If you want to go to the hospital I'll drive you."

"No. She's sleeping, apparently. I'll phone the daughter tomorrow." He rubbed at his chin, grimacing, and muttered something she didn't catch. "Excuse me." He consulted his watch, then looked up a number in the notebook and dialed it. From the brief conversation that followed she gathered he was ordering flowers for the housekeeper.

"Are you fond of her?" Riley asked when he'd finished. "Has she been with you a long time?"

"Nearly four years, and we get along. She's excellent at her job and a great cook—dammit."

"Dammit?"

"I'm expecting guests for a dinner Mrs. Hardy was apparently preparing when she fell. I'll have to find a caterer at short notice or book a table in a restaurant."

"What will happen to the food your housekeeper was going to serve?"

"If it can't be frozen or something, I'll throw it

out, I suppose." He sounded as if that was the least of his worries.

"That's a terrible waste! How many people are you expecting?"

"Seven." He held the pencil in two fingers, absently drumming it on the papers.

"I suppose you don't cook." She tried not to sound critical.

"Not well enough for this." He closed the folder and stretched his legs out over the briefcase, then lapsed into silence.

When she pulled up at his house he turned to her. "If any of that food's any use to you, you're welcome to it."

"That's generous of you."

"I don't like waste, either."

She followed him along a broad path between immaculately mown lawns and onto the tiled front porch that was almost a carriageway. He pressed a button on his key tag, inserted a key into a polished brass lock and pushed open the huge paneled door.

Benedict parked his briefcase under a telephone table standing on a pale marble floor. "The kitchen's through here," he said, leading her along a red-and-black carpet runner that looked sumptuous against the gold-flecked marble.

Louvered saloon doors opened at his touch, displaying gleaming ceramic tiles and stainless steel.

An enormous refrigerator stood next to a matching upright freezer, and a bumpy cotton cloth covered a table in the center of the room. Riley deduced someone had hastily thrown it over the food preparations.

Benedict said, "Have a look and see what's there." He turned to another telephone on the wall, pulled out a volume of yellow pages from the phone books sitting beneath it and began leafing through.

Riley lifted the cloth, peeking at mounds of vegetables and a bowl of flour, a block of cheese, some serving plates—and an open recipe book.

Benedict dialed a number, then put his hand over the mouthpiece. "Look in the fridge and the pantry too. It's over there. Anything that'll spoil, you're welcome to—yes, hello?" He turned to speak into the receiver. "Could you do a dinner party at short notice?"

Riley went into the pantry, which was about the size of a normal kitchen and was stacked with packets and cans and bottles, and wire baskets of vegetables. She took a couple of neatly folded plastic bags from a shelf, returned to the kitchen and opened the refrigerator, finding chicken pieces in a marinade, a couple of dozen oysters in their shells, and a covered dish of raw cubed fish in lemon juice.

Benedict was dialing another number. "Hello, I need a rush job...tonight.... I understand, thanks anyway."

Holding the phone, Benedict was running a finger down the page in front of him. Riley lifted the cover from the table, folding it back.

Benedict slammed the receiver back on its hook, letting fly an expletive that made her turn her head.

"An answering machine." He returned to his perusal of the phone book, and reached again for the handset. "Hello? Yes...can you do a dinner party tonight? Yes, I did say tonight. I know, but— A nice evening to you too."

When he cut the connection, Riley stifled a giggle. "You mean," she suggested, "May your soup be watery, your main dish burnt to a crisp and your dessert melt on its way to the table.''

Benedict gave a reluctant laugh. "Something like that. I might have better luck with restaurants.''

As he closed the book and reached for its companion volume, she said, "Why don't I do it?''

"I'm capable of finding a decent restaurant, thanks.''

She cast him an impatient look. "I mean I could cook dinner for you—call it a part payment for the repair to your car.''

"You?''

"I can cook. Ask my roommates. I mean housemates." She still had trouble with some Kiwi idioms.

"This is a bit different from cooking for your housemates, Riley.''

"I know." She decided to ignore his patronizing tone. "But with these ingredients—'' she indicated the laden table "—I promise you I can do it. I even know what Mrs. Whatsit was going to cook.''

"Mrs. Hardy,'' he said automatically. "This dinner party is rather important to me. I really don't think—''

"I've worked in restaurants.'' She wasn't a great academic, but she was good at picking things up by watching, and some of the chefs had encouraged her desire to learn. "If you're not satisfied you don't need to pay me—or rather, I'll still pay you. Do you want me to serve, as well?''

"Mrs. Hardy would have, but—''

"Okay." She put down the plastic bags. "I won't turn up in your dining room like this,'' she assured him, catching his dubious survey of her. "I've got decent clothes in the car. Oh, you'd better show me where the dining room is. You'll want the table set if Mrs. Hardy hasn't already done it.''

"Don't you have responsibilities of your own?" he said slowly. "I mean, what about your—"

"Nothing to worry about," she said breezily. "If I can use that phone, I'll just let my housemates know I'll be late home." It was Harry's turn to provide dinner and he usually bought a take-out meal, anyway. Purposefully she moved toward the phone.

Benedict shifted aside. "Won't you need to arrange—"

She put a hand on his chest and gave him a small, reassuring pat before she picked up the phone and began dialing. "Look, it's not your problem, okay? But it will help to solve mine if you let me take it off what I owe you. Tell you what," she added, fishing Snoopy and her keys from her pocket, "you could go and get the bag that's on the back seat, for me. It's got my good clothes in it."

Looking rather stunned, he took the keys from her, opened his mouth to say something, closed it again and walked out.

By the time he returned with the cheap shopping bag, Riley had realized how she'd spoken to him, and as she hung up the phone she said guiltily, "I'm sorry—I treated you like one of my housemates, didn't I, instead of my employer for the night? Thanks, anyway."

"Is it okay with them, then?"

"No worries." She took the bag and peeked into it.

"I suppose it's handy to be living with other people."

"Yes," she said, rummaging in the bag for the

blouse and skirt. She could never afford a place on her own, and she'd been lucky that they got on so well. "I'll need to borrow an iron later. I hope these'll be all right?" She held the clothes roughly against her and looked at him anxiously.

Benedict cleared his throat. "They'll be fine. You looked very nice this morning. The iron's in the laundry, through there." He indicated the direction. "Look, it's a bit much, throwing you into this. I can help if you tell me what to do."

She wondered if he had an ulterior motive, like keeping an eye on her to ensure she really could do what she claimed and still leaving himself the last-minute option of a restaurant. But she smiled unoffendedly at him and said, "I'll let you know. Now, where's the dining room?"

"Uh..." For a minute she was afraid he'd decided to turn down her offer after all. His eyes had gone glassy. Then he seemed to give himself a little shake, a fine tremor running over his hard-muscled body inside the sharp business suit. "This way," he said.

Chapter Three

Riley left Benedict putting plates and cutlery on the big dining table and hurried away to the kitchen.

When he came back she was slicing onions. "I thought I'd serve the oysters au naturel with lemon wedges," she said, pausing to wipe her forearm over her eyes, "and arrange them around the fish salad."

"Sounds fine."

"What about wine?"

"I'll deal with that."

He probably wouldn't have trusted her with it, anyway. Not that she often got a chance to sample good wine, but she did know enough to bluff her way through a wine list.

"Glasses," she said, sniffing as she tipped the onions into a dish. They were very strong. "I couldn't find wine goblets."

"They're kept in a cabinet in the dining room, and I've already put them on the table. Do you want a tissue or something?"

"Thanks, I'm okay." She turned to rinse her hands and then eyes at the tap.

When she raised her head he was standing beside her with a paper towel ready. Riley took it from him and blotted her face. "Ta." Raising her reddened eyes to him, she was surprised to see him looking back at her rather fixedly, his own eyes dark and intense.

Riley blinked again, uncertainly. Her tongue crept unconsciously to her crooked tooth, parting her lips.

Benedict's black brows drew together, and he stepped back. "What else do you want done?" he asked, looking at the table.

"Um…" For some reason she felt a bit breathless. She walked jerkily to the stainless steel lidded bin near the twin sinks, dropping the crumpled paper towel into it. "You could get a tin of coconut cream from the pantry for me. I can't reach it."

"Whereabouts in the pantry?"

"I'll show you." She led the way, stood in front of the shelf where she'd seen the tins, and pointed. "There."

"One tin?" He reached past her to lift it down.

Riley felt him brush her shoulder, and moved aside. "Thanks." Taking the tin, she glanced up to find him smiling slightly, a disconcerting gleam in his eyes. "What?"

"You wouldn't want to know," he said mysteriously. "Do you need any more help?"

He found, fetched, grated and chopped at her behest. When savory aromas began to seep into the room from the wall oven, and Riley was piling used bowls and saucepans into the sink, he glanced at his watch and said, "Anything else? And by the way, there's a dishwasher for those."

She looked at the white machine under the counter. "These things will take up a lot of room, and I can wash them in five minutes."

"As you like. I should go and change before my guests arrive. The downstairs bathroom is all yours. Next to the laundry."

"I'll clean up and change when I've done the washing up. Do you want me to answer the door?"

"No, just look after the food."

When he'd gone upstairs Riley inspected the table setting, straightening some knives and adding condiments, then ran an iron over her blouse and skirt and had a quick shower in the small but elegant marble bathroom, using one of the fluffy peach-colored towels she found on a brass shelf. She combed her hair and wove the strands into a braid before winding her hair tie round the end. It looked neat and efficient, she hoped.

She put out fresh hand towels for the guests and hurried back to the kitchen. Finding a full-length apron hanging on the back of the pantry door, she dropped it about her neck, and tied the strings firmly at her waist. Also behind the door was a folded step stool. She wondered if Benedict Falkner even knew it was there.

The apron fell below her skirt, and the broad band around her neck was far too big, making the top flop into a pouch, but it was also too wide to knot.

She found a short, sturdy knife and began shucking oysters, laying them in their half shells around the edge of a large serving platter.

Benedict returned in a cream shirt and a dark-red

figured waistcoat with black trousers. He looked stunning.

Carefully Riley laid the lemon wedge in her hand onto a nest of green fennel between the last two oysters, and picked up a tiny carrot rosette from the dozen or so she'd made.

"Very impressive," Benedict said. "You said you'd worked in restaurants—where?"

"New York, a couple of places in England, and here."

Deftly she was placing more rosettes.

"How long were you in America? I thought I detected an accent."

"I went to high school there, and college." She moved the completed dish out of the way and pulled another toward her. "I was born in New Zealand while Dad was working in agricultural research here, but my parents are American. Hand me that bowl of chives?"

Passing it, Benedict looked down at her, and the skin around his eyes crinkled. "You look like a kid wearing her mother's apron."

So much for the hairstyle. Riley yanked up the top of the apron, but it immediately flopped again. "Do me a favor," she said, pulling apart the bow at her waist. "If you can loop one of the strings through the neck bit and tie it again..."

She turned her back to allow him to do it. It took him a while, and she could feel his breath stirring her hair as he fumbled with the bow, even hear him breathing, but finally he said, "Okay?"

"Thank you." The bib of the apron came to the base of her neck but it was more comfortable, and she no longer resembled a kangaroo. "I've made a platter of hors d'oeuvres—shall I bring it into the lounge when your guests arrive?''

"I'll take it through now. They should be here any minute.''

Over the next thirty minutes the bell rang three times, and Riley heard voices in the hall, becoming muted as the guests moved into the lounge.

It was some time before Benedict pushed through the swing doors. ''When can we eat?''

"Is fifteen minutes okay?''

"Yep.'' He crossed to the fridge to take out a couple of bottles of wine before he left again.

Exactly fifteen minutes later Riley pulled off the apron and carried the oysters, now surrounding a glass bowl of coconut-cream-drenched fish salad, into the dining room, along with two silver baskets of breads cut into wedges.

Everyone was already seated around the long table. Benedict poured wine into a glass set in front of a young woman seated to his right, who inclined her head in order to catch something he was saying, her sky-blue eyes fixed on him. Thick, loose blond curls fell about an exquisite face without a freckle or a blemish, and her mouth was the kind that men were supposed to find irresistible—pouting and lush and painted a bright poppy pink.

Her neck was smooth and graceful and she had real cleavage, not too blatantly shown off by a shoestring-strapped dress that matched her lipstick and played up a faint, glowing tan. That simple-looking little dress had probably cost more than a month of Riley's wages.

Riley hated her on sight. The woman wasn't an inch below five-six, she suspected, and utterly gor-

geous. In high heels she'd be about as tall as Benedict—maybe taller, Riley guessed hopefully as she
leaned over the table between two other guests, just
stopping herself from plonking down the platter with
a thud. Instead she slid it gently onto the cloth, placed
the bread baskets on either side of it and stepped
back.

Benedict looked up. "Thank you, Riley." He gave
her the glimmer of a conspiratorial smile.

As she left, a light, feminine voice said, "Where's
Mrs. Hardy, Benedict?"

That voice had been trained at one of Auckland's
best private schools—Riley would have taken a bet
on it—and she just knew who it belonged to.

Already on her way back to the kitchen, she
couldn't hear Benedict's reply.

Taking in the next dishes, she deliberately refrained
from looking at either Benedict or the blonde.

The other guests were a middle-aged pair and two
thirtyish couples. Riley gathered from the conversation as she went in and out, clearing and serving, that
the older people were the blonde young woman's parents, that *her* name was Tiffany, and that Benedict
had some sort of business connection with the family.
The thirty-somethings were obviously friends of his,
and they too had that air of sleek well-being and sophistication that came with money.

When Riley had served dessert—a quickly made
chilled specialty of her own involving fruit and
whipped cream and topped with freshly toasted sliv-
ered almonds—she stopped by Benedict's chair.
"Would you like your coffee served here?"

Tiffany interjected, "Oh, let's have it on the terrace! It's lovely out there. And it isn't too cold, is it?''

Everyone agreed that it wasn't too cold, and Benedict nodded to Riley. "On the terrace, then." He indicated the broad tiled area outside the dining room, where several canvas chairs and a couple of loungers were grouped. A palette-shaped swimming pool gleamed and glittered under outdoor lighting set among glossy shrubs.

Riley was placing cups on a tray when she looked up to see Tiffany's face above the center curve of the saloon doors before they parted and the young woman carried in a pile of emptied dessert plates. "Can I help?" she asked. "It was a magnificent meal. That wonderful dessert is going to be awfully bad for my figure though!"

"Thank you," Riley said. Darn, the woman was *nice!* In addition to the hair and the face and the cleavage, and the long legs that Riley would have killed for. And she wouldn't be taller than Benedict. Just about on a level, in her heels.

Tiffany crossed to the dishwashing machine and opened it. "Benedict had two helpings. I suppose you wouldn't give me the recipe?" she asked, loading in spoons and plates.

Riley swallowed. "Yes, of course. Do you want to write it down?" She looked toward the telephone where a grocery pad and pen hung.

"*Thank* you!" Tiffany grabbed the pen, tore off a blank page and sat down at the table.

Riley dictated the simple recipe while she waited for the coffee machine to finish doing its thing.

"Is that all?" Tiffany looked up as Riley finished.

She folded the paper and jumped up. "Now, can I carry something for you?"

They took the coffee, cream and sugar to the terrace where the others waited, and then Riley finished clearing the table and returned to the kitchen to make more coffee and clean up.

She washed the wineglasses separately, placing them on the kitchen table to be put away when the guests had left.

Maybe she should ask if they needed more coffee. Percolator in hand, she was heading for the door when Tiffany came back with the empty pot. "Great minds." The girl beamed. "Just pour it into this and I'll take it out."

She was very much at home here, Riley thought, watching her retreat down the passageway. Benedict's girlfriend, she supposed.

Suddenly tired, she could do with a coffee herself. Maybe she could sneak out the back way when she drank it. Benedict surely didn't need her anymore, and she had no idea how late his dinner guests might stay.

Indistinct voices floated down the passageway, and she heard a door close.

While she was pouring herself coffee, Benedict came in. He carried the tray, piled with cups and liqueur glasses.

"Do you want me to wash those up?" she asked him.

"No." He parked the tray on the counter. "You've done enough. Have you had anything to eat, yourself?"

"I snacked on leftovers, and I'm just having some coffee—" She still held the percolator.

"I'll join you." He grabbed a cup from a rack and came over with it, holding it out for her to fill.

"Your guests have all gone?"

"Yes, they're gone." He sat down at the table with her.

"Was everything, um, satisfactory?" she asked anxiously.

"Everything was fine." He smiled at her. "They were very impressed. And so am I. Thank you."

"I owed you. I'll pick you up again tomorrow morning," she said. "You won't have your car until the afternoon, will you?"

"After what you've done tonight you'll be tired. I can make other arrangements."

"I said I would transport you until it's fixed," she reminded him. "I'll be here on time."

"You always do what you say you will?" he queried, glancing curiously at her.

"I try not to make promises I can't keep."

"Me too." He looked at her for longer this time, in a thoughtful, almost absentminded manner.

Riley shifted her gaze, lifting her cup to sip the coffee. It was too hot, and she hastily put it down again. "Your girlfriend's nice," she said, idly turning the cup.

"My...girlfriend?"

She looked up. "Isn't Tiffany...?"

He answered in a rather odd tone. "Not yet."

Riley's heart did something very peculiar. A sort of flip upward, followed by a downward plunge. Of course she knew hearts didn't really do that sort of thing, but that's what it felt like. She swallowed, staring down at the steam rising from her cup. "You do like her, though?"

Maybe he needed to think about it, because he didn't answer immediately. Then he said decisively, as if he'd just made up his mind, "Yes, I do. I like her very much."

"I'm sorry about jumping to conclusions," Riley said. "Only she seemed to know her way around...the kitchen."

"She's been here before."

"She's very pretty," Riley said forlornly. "Beautiful."

"Yes," he agreed. "Very."

And not short of a cent or two—or at least her parents must be well off. Absolutely up to Benedict Falkner's standard.

She picked up her coffee again and gulped some, regardless of the fact that it burned on the way down. "There are lots of leftovers." Her voice was husky, probably because of her seared throat. "Do you want me to put some in the freezer?"

Benedict drank some of his own coffee. "Why don't you take them home?"

"If you're sure you don't want them, thanks. I could bring the containers back in the morning."

"Anytime." He put his cup down and stared at the table, looking suddenly discontented.

"Is something the matter?"

After a moment he glanced up. "No, of course not." He sounded slightly impatient, and she bit her lip. It was none of her business, in other words.

Maybe Tiffany was playing hard to get. After all, she seemed to know him—or at least his house—quite well, and yet he'd said she wasn't his girlfriend. Yet.

Riley's heart sank still further. She finished her coffee and stood up to take the cup to the sink. "Sure you don't want me to wash these?"

"I'll do it," he said. "Tomorrow."

"I was going to put away the glasses."

"Leave them. Will you be all right getting home?"

"I'll be fine." He probably wanted to get rid of her.

"You look tired," he said critically, studying her face as she turned away from the sink. "I could call you a taxi."

Right. Tiffany looked beautiful, Riley just looked tired. "I can still drive," she said a little tartly.

He walked her out to the car, and she drove away with a strange hollow feeling in her chest.

When she dragged herself out of bed in the morning, she still looked tired. After putting on a reasonably respectable pair of jeans and a fairly new ribbed-knit top that hugged her slight figure, she rummaged in a drawer for a lipstick and dashed it over her mouth.

It only made her cheeks look paler. Blotting most of it off left a smidgen of color, and she combed her hair back from her face and fastened it with a giant butterfly clip before leaving the house.

At Benedict's place she climbed out of the car and went to the porch with the pile of containers she'd washed after transferring the contents the previous night.

Benedict opened the door and she said, "I brought these back—shall I take them through to the kitchen?"

He had his briefcase in one hand, the newspaper in

the other. "Just put them on the telephone table there."

When she had done so and turned to where he was waiting at the door, she discovered that he was watching her with a rather surprised expression, his gaze fixed on her torso.

He gestured for her to precede him, and she walked past him, catching the faint masculine scent that she'd come to associate with him.

Lightly she ran down the steps and walked along the path. The back of her neck prickled as she heard his footsteps behind her. Head high, she was unusually conscious of the way the jeans clung to her hips and her neat behind. She sometimes shopped in the children's section for her clothes as they were less likely to be too big in the waist or too long, but they tended not to allow for a grown woman's more rounded figure.

In the car, Benedict opened the paper and was soon immersed in it.

Feeling for some reason more and more depressed, Riley drove silently. Last night they'd been almost friendly, preparing dinner together, getting in each other's way occasionally, talking. He'd tied her apron for her, and had laughed secretly at some private joke that he'd refused to share. Riley strongly suspected he'd found it amusing that she couldn't reach the shelf herself—by the average person's standards it wasn't all that high.

He'd even sat companionably drinking coffee with her at the end of the evening. But now Benedict seemed to be deliberately distancing himself from the hired help.

Not fair, Riley scolded herself. She'd volunteered

to drive him, offered to help him out last night, and she was probably getting the best of the deal. He'd tacitly agreed that the catering would go toward reducing her debt.

Which ought to make her happy.

"How is Mrs. Hardy?" she enquired.

"She's resting at her daughter's home and feeling much better, she says."

Maybe she'd be back at work soon. Riley pulled up in Benedict's office car park with a jerk, and muttered, "Sorry."

"Thanks for the lift." He refolded the newspaper and undid his seat belt. "You can keep the paper if you like. And thanks again for last night, Riley. You saved my bacon—or chicken."

"That's all right." She could be offhand too. "Sure you don't want me tonight?"

Benedict's brows lifted and his lips twitched at the corners.

Riley said hastily, "I mean, you don't want to be picked up after work?"

Sounding rather distant, he confirmed, "I won't be needing you again."

"Right. Then if you send me the bill for your car, I'll start paying it off. You can deduct whatever last night was worth to you." She held out her hand. "Thank you for being so decent about things. Goodbye."

"Goodbye," he said slowly, and took her hand in his. His clasp was warm and firm. And it didn't last long enough.

But unexpectedly he bent close and brushed a kiss across her mouth, his lips lingering for a second with a slight pressure before he drew back. And then he swung himself out of the car and shut the door.

It wasn't a real kiss, Riley told herself, stunned and somehow bereft. Lots of people kiss on the lips in a social context. And lots of men will kiss a woman friend rather than shake hands. It doesn't mean a thing.

But her lips were tingling, and there was a fluttery excitement in her throat.

Damn, but Benedict Falkner was attractive. Did he know just how attractive?

Probably. He'd sounded pretty confident when he'd said that Tiffany wasn't his girlfriend...*yet*.

Remembering Tiffany, Riley forced herself to accept reality. There was no way she could compete with *that*.

For a minute or two this morning Benedict might have noticed dimly that she was a woman, that she had a figure—such as it was. But it didn't mean he was going to transfer his attention from a golden creature like Tiffany to a brown mouse like Riley.

Her mouth curved in a wry smile. Fat chance.

It wasn't as if she could transform herself like the heroine in some old films who took off her owlish glasses, shook out her hair from its tight bun into a halo of bouncy curls, opened a button or two on her prissy office-type blouse and instantly became a raving beauty.

Riley didn't need glasses and, shaken or not, her hair remained determinedly fine and straight and far from bouncy, refusing to hold a curl even when permed. For a little while she'd used a color rinse but the ''Copper Glow'' seemed to echo the freckles on her nose, making them more noticeable, and anyway she couldn't be bothered using the stuff every time she washed her hair.

Best forget about Benedict Falkner. Ten to one— *twenty* to one—the man would forget about her soon enough. There wouldn't even be a visible scratch on his shiny, expensive car to remind him.

Harry's daughter came to stay for the weekend. Rosalita was almost a year old, a chubby charmer with round, nearly black eyes, sooty curls and a throaty chuckle. Harry adored her, and his house-mates spoiled her whenever she visited.

Late on Saturday morning Logie mowed the lawns while Riley, Harry and Lin washed up the dishes no one had mustered the energy to do the previous night, and Samuela energetically used the vacuum cleaner.

When Rosalita began investigating the kitchen cup-boards, Riley picked up the baby to distract her from her firm intention to empty the shelves.

"We'll finish up the dishes," Harry offered, "if you can keep her out of here for ten minutes."

Riley carried her into the wide hallway, shutting the door behind them. A jumble of toys lay on the faded carpet runner, and she gave a striped ball a gentle kick, put down the child and initiated a game of chase the ball.

Rosalita had just begun to toddle, but she was faster on hands and knees. Riley followed suit, and soon had Rosalita giggling while they crawled at speed down the long carpet runner in pursuit of the ball.

It bounced against the front door, and Rosalita cap-tured it, hugging it to her as she sat back. Then the doorbell rang and Riley picked the baby up, scrambling to her feet. The ball fell to the floor and rolled away as she opened the door.

The baby balanced on her hip, Riley blinked against the sunlight from outside, pushing a hank of hair from her eyes, and looked up at the man standing there.

"Hello, Riley," Benedict Falkner said.

Damn, she was wearing baggy-kneed leggings and a faded T-shirt, her feet were bare, and her hair was in its usual mess.

"Hi," she said, brazening it out.

"Man!" Rosalita pronounced knowingly, pointing at Benedict with a chubby finger.

Riley grinned. "Yeah, I think so. This is Rosalita," she told Benedict as the baby grabbed at her hair. "Come on in."

She stepped back and he accepted the invitation, standing by as she closed the door. Rosalita began to chew the lock of hair she held, mumbling, "Mmm-umm-mmm-muh!" Carefully Riley removed it from her mouth and pried the tiny but tenacious fingers away.

Benedict looked from her to the child and back again, his face going rather wooden. Maybe he didn't like children.

"I...ah...brought this along for you," he said, withdrawing an envelope from his pocket.

Harry came out of the kitchen.

"Dadda!" Rosalita beamed as if she hadn't seen him in an age, holding out her arms.

"Right, go to your daddy," Riley said, giving the child a quick kiss on her silky curls before transferring her to Harry's willing arms. Samuela hauled the vacuum cleaner into the hall, looked up to say hi to

Benedict and went on pushing the nozzle over the carpet.

"Come into the sitting room," Riley said to Benedict over the whine of the machine. "Would you like a coffee or something?"

"Thanks, no."

He followed her, and she motioned him to a chair as she lowered herself to the comfortable old sofa. A huge, gangly stuffed rabbit with a bald stomach and one ear missing sprawled beside her.

She opened the envelope he'd given her and read the single sheet of paper. Scrawled across it was "Paid in Full," followed by a sprawling, purposeful signature—"B. Falkner."

She said, puzzled, "This isn't the panel beater's bill."

"Your debt is canceled," he said. "That dinner would have cost me more than you owed."

"Are you sure?" She should have been elated. Instead she felt oddly flat. She shuffled her bare feet on the worn carpet. "How much was the bill?" She suspected he was being generous. "Um, I did say I'd reimburse you."

"Forget it. What you did was worth every cent."

He obviously wasn't going to budge. "Well, thanks," she said lamely.

There was an awkward little silence. "So this is where you live." Benedict looked about the big, shabby room, with a cheap TV set in one corner, a discarded newspaper on the floor by one of the armchairs, and a set of planks separated by an assortment of bricks and stone blocks serving as bookshelves for the housemates' eclectic selection of reading matter.

"We like it," Riley said shortly, acutely aware of the contrast between this and his upmarket house.

"I wasn't criticizing," he said mildly. His gaze lingered on a large, battered garden gnome with a demented stare, standing guard over the empty fireplace. A red Santa sock was pulled over its pointed plaster hat.

"That's Homer," Riley told him.

"Homer?"

"Logie found him in the streetside inorganic waste collection and persuaded us to give him a home."

Enlightened, Benedict nodded. "He was obviously traumatized by his experience."

Riley picked up the rabbit and absently hugged it to her, her fingers playing with the remaining ear. "Um...how's Mrs. Hardy?"

He was looking at the rabbit now. "That thing's almost as big as you are." Raising his eyes to her, he said, "Mrs. Hardy's feeling fine, but it *was* a small stroke she had, and her daughter's persuaded her to give up work and go to live with her permanently."

"So...how are you managing?"

"At the moment I'm using a cleaning service and eating out a lot. I've interviewed a few people, but so far I'm not happy about any of them."

"Fussy, are you?"

"I guess so." Abruptly he stood up. "I'd better go."

Probably he couldn't wait to get back to his own milieu where he felt comfortable.

Lin poked her head around the door. "Riley...oh! I didn't know you had a visitor. Where's Rosalita?"

"Harry's got her," Riley said, and Lin disappeared.

"He's…uh…very good-looking," Benedict said.

"Harry? Yes he is." Harry's mix'n'match forebears had endowed him with impressive genes. He supplemented his income from driving a courier van with part-time modeling, and lifted weights for a hobby.

"When you mentioned housemates, I didn't realize—" She waited for him to finish but instead he cleared his throat and said, "Well…that's it then."

He moved out of the room, and Riley trailed behind him. "It was nice of you to come over," she said. He could have posted the receipt.

He looked back at her over his shoulder and accidentally kicked the discarded ball. It bounced off the opposite wall across the floor, forcing Riley to take evasive action. Skipping aside, she blundered into Benedict, and his hands closed on her shoulders.

For a second she was held close to him, felt the hardness of his chest against her breasts, his chin brushing her temple. And that faint scent tantalized her nostrils.

Then he released her, leaving her breathless and disoriented, and was on his way to the front door, walking fast.

Riley was behind him when he opened it. She waited while he stepped out onto the porch, the loose board that Logie was always promising to fix creaking under his feet. A peal of baby giggles came from the window of Harry's room, followed by Harry's deep laughter.

Benedict paused, turned to Riley and gave her a strange, searching look. "He's Tamati's father too?"

Riley's jaw dropped half a mile. "*Harry?* Whatever made you ask me that?'' Somewhere he'd got his wires badly crossed.

"Sorry,'' he said curtly. "It's none of my business how many children you have, or who fathered them. Goodbye, Riley.''

you think you got the last of them, another tiny
batch wriggles to life.

"Lots of luck," she said, unwilling to involve herself even further in...the week's...he looked though
Chapter to relax.

Chapter Four

He was halfway down the steps before Riley shut
her gaping mouth and found her voice. "Benedict!"

Benedict paused, then turned. "Yes?" His gaze
flickered to her face, before his eyelids lowered, and
he thrust a hand into a pocket of his slacks. With one
foot on the path, another on the step, he looked impatient to be going.

She didn't suppose he cared, but...."They're not
mine," she said.

"What?" Benedict frowned.

"I don't have any children."

"You don't...Tamati?"

"Tamati's one of the children at the day care center
where I work," Riley explained.

"You work at a day care center?" He was looking
at her fully now, almost as if he didn't believe her.

"Yes. Um...not that it matters, I guess."

He was looking fixedly at her. "Of course it
doesn't matter." She thought a deeper color had come

into his cheeks. "But I apologize," he said, "for jumping to conclusions."

"That's all right," she returned mechanically.

He hesitated, and their eyes met. "Ah...Rosalita's mother, then...?" he queried.

"Harry asked her to marry him when she found out she was pregnant, but she said no. They have a friendly arrangement—but they're not together anymore."

"So...are you?"

"Me?"

"You and Harry."

Riley blinked, then laughed. "No!"

Benedict stepped fully onto the path, shoved the other hand into a pocket, and rocked a little on his heels. He withdrew his gaze, looking about as if searching for something—a change of subject, maybe. Or a graceful way to say goodbye. Finally he returned his attention to her and asked, "Are you still job hunting?"

Looking down at a man was a novel experience for Riley. She savored it for a moment. "Yes." She grimaced. "Not much luck, though."

"Then...maybe I have a proposition for you."

"P-proposition?"

"Would you be interested in filling Mrs. Hardy's place?"

"Me?"

"You did say you'd take any job, but maybe housekeeping isn't your thing."

The flat wasn't that bad, was it? He hadn't even seen the kitchen... "I'm not a professional, but I guess I could..."

"And if you would drive me sometimes. Not having to drive myself lets me get a bit of extra work done on the journey, and that could be useful when I'm pressed for time." He went on rapidly, "It's a live-in position, rent-free, and food provided. Two days off a week, plus any other time that you aren't needed, but sometimes you'd be working nights and weekends."

"I could have some mornings off for classes?"

"No problem. We can work out the exact hours."

"So…what are you paying?" she asked, trying to be pragmatic. This sounded too good to be true. He was probably offering slave wages.

When he told her, she was hard put not to let her mouth fall open again. "All that and *real money* too?" she couldn't help saying.

Benedict laughed. "In my experience you get what you pay for. I ask a lot from my staff and reward them well for it." He paused, then said offhandedly, "Think it over, and if you're interested we'll talk."

Who wouldn't be interested? It was a dream job, at least on the surface. "Is there a catch?" She was finding it difficult to believe that something like that could just fall into her lap.

Benedict seemed to grow suddenly taller, his face setting in forbidding lines. "No strings," he said tersely. "The housekeeper has a separate suite near the kitchen, and I promise you'll be quite safe. There's even a lock."

"I didn't mean that!" Of course she'd be safe—he had the gorgeous Tiffany, or at least he intended to have her. And no doubt his pick of other equally gorgeous women who moved in his own social circle, if he wanted them. He didn't need to cast his eye in the direction of someone like Riley. "It sounds great," she said. "Thank you for offering it to me."

"But, no thanks?"

"I didn't say that!" In fact she ought to leap at it, and she wasn't sure why she was being uncharacteristically cautious about this. "You did tell me to think it over."

He relaxed a little. "Do that. If you have any questions, give me a call. You still have my number?"

"Yes. I'll be in touch."

"Right." He swung round and headed off to his car, parked on the roadside.

Riley watched him drive away, wondering if she ought to pinch herself to make sure she was actually awake.

Her housemates helped her compile a list of questions she should ask. Expected hours of work, days off, space for her car, holidays...

"He's not after your body, is he?" Lin gave her a half-humorous, half-anxious look as they lay on Riley's bed, sharing a packet of potato crisps.

"No such luck." Riley popped another crisp into her mouth.

Lin laughed. "Oh, are you after his? You did say he was luscious."

"At first glance," Riley agreed cautiously.

And second and third, fourth, fifth...

She hadn't even realized she'd been counting. A faint apprehension coiled in her stomach. But it would be stupid to turn down a fabulous job just because her employer happened to be one of the sexiest men she'd ever seen. It wasn't as though he'd shown any interest in her. And her unsurprising interest in him was akin to lusting after a film star or pop musician, no more than a pleasant fantasy. "Did I tell you about Tiffany?" she asked Lin.

"Who's Tiffany?"

Riley told her about Tiffany. "Anyway, after a few weeks of picking up after him in the bathroom and washing his socks and underpants I don't suppose I'll find him nearly such a turn-on," she concluded hopefully.

He wasn't the first good-looking male to cross her path, and she had never been the type to lose her head over a man. Maybe it came from being brought up with brothers—the other sex held no particular mystery for her.

The following evening Riley phoned Benedict and went through the list, trying not to notice that over the phone his voice was like melted dark chocolate and reminding herself that this was strictly business.

"Whichever two days off you prefer," he said. "Mrs. Hardy took Sunday and Tuesday, but I hope you'll be flexible because some weekends I'm entertaining. Mrs. Hardy and I always managed to work things out." Three weeks' annual leave, a month's notice on either side of termination of her employment, and she could park her car in the three-car garage.

Riley pictured her shabby Corona alongside the shiny BMW. He was probably biting his tongue to stop himself from telling her to be careful. "Will I need a uniform?" she asked, ticking the last item off her list.

Benedict laughed. "What you had on the other night looked fine to me. And unless I have guests I don't care what you wear. What else do you need to know?''

''Um...I think that's all. Won't you need references or something?''

''References.'' His voice turned brisk. ''If you could come over tomorrow evening and bring them with you, I'll read them, and you can inspect the accommodation and have a look around the house.''

He opened the door to her wearing a business shirt with the sleeves unevenly half-rolled, and dark trousers but no tie. His salon haircut looked faintly disheveled, as though he'd been running his fingers through it.

''Hi,'' he said, and smiled at her. That smile was to die for, and her answering one was a trifle strained.

He led her to a room lined with built-in shelves. A wide desk and a big swivel chair behind it faced a window looking over a lawn at the back of the house. A tiled path curving through cleverly planted shrubs gave an illusion of distance to a small, latticed, pagoda-shaped building tucked among slender birches and covered with climbing vines.

Benedict set a straight chair for her, and perched on the edge of the desk as she pulled a slim bundle of papers from her bag. ''I figured you'd be more interested in local references, but I've brought a couple of others.''

He quickly glanced through, then refolded them and gave them back, giving her a searching look. ''They all mention how well you relate to people. Maybe you'll find it boring here on your own.''

''On my days off I can see my friends, and...could

I invite them here if we keep to my part of the house?''

"Of course." He cast her an enigmatic glance, and his voice turned almost austere. "Who you entertain in your own time is up to you. The suite has a private walled patio, but Mrs. Hardy kept the gate from that to the garden locked after she found an intruder lurking there. You'd probably be wise to do the same, at least at night, although the alarm system should stop a break-in. The other access is through the kitchen. I'll show you the suite now.''

The two rooms weren't large, but the cozy furnished lounge looked comfortable, with a TV set and a telephone, and the sheltered patio was delightful. The bedroom, facing the same direction as his study, had a long dressing table shelf that would double nicely as a desk, and two single beds with matching cream covers.

The compact private bathroom was sheer luxury. No more waiting in the cold to be next into the shower on a winter morning, or banging on the door and hurrying up Logie or Samuela when she was running late. No more ancient pipes announcing every bathroom visit through her bedroom wall.

"The two-seater sofa opens to a double bed," Benedict told her as they retraced their steps through the sitting room. "Mrs. Hardy used it when her grandchildren stayed overnight.''

The house was built on several intersecting levels. The formal lounge overlooked the pool, but a smaller sitting room on another level had glass doors to one of the balconies and the spiral wrought-iron staircase that led to the garden. On the top floor Benedict threw open the doors to four bedrooms and two bathrooms.

In the master bedroom a padded brocade throw patterned in black and brown with touches of gold covered a low, wide bed, matching the full-length drapes framing a door to a smaller balcony.

A paperback thriller lay facedown on one of the mahogany bedside tables, and a stack of books with library numbers on them sat beside it. At least the man relaxed sometimes.

As they descended the curved staircase to the marble-floored entrance hall, Benedict said, "Most of the time I'm the only one here, though occasionally I have overnight guests."

Girlfriends? Well, surely she could cope with that. "Who does the garden?" she asked.

"A man mows the lawns once a week, and when I have time I tackle the weeds and trim shrubs, but if I'm too busy he does that too. You'd only be expected to care for the house." Reaching the floor level, he turned as she paused on the bottom step.

Riley took a deep breath. "I'd like to take the job."

He didn't say anything for a moment, and she wondered if he'd changed his mind. But then he said, "When can you start?"

"The day care center needs two weeks' notice, but I could move in right away," Riley offered. "Tomorrow, if you like."

Benedict looked pleased. "Great. I have to entertain a client and his wife on Wednesday evening. I'd planned to book a restaurant table, but if you could manage dinner…?"

"I'll cook it after I come back from the day care center, and I'll do a bit of basic housework." She'd do the bulk of it on Wednesdays when she didn't have classes, and a quick tidy up the other days, until she'd worked out her notice at the center.

"I'll draw up an employment contract and give you a key. I'm usually out Tuesday nights."

She left her wardrobe and bed behind, on the understanding that if her replacement tenant didn't want to buy them she'd advertise them for sale, and packed her things into boxes.

"Wow!" Logie unbent after putting down Riley's personal music center in her new sitting room and looked around. "All *right!*"

Harry carried in a large cardboard carton. "Where do you want this?"

Peering at it, Riley said, "Bedroom. Through there."

When everything had been brought in, she made coffee in the big kitchen and carried it through to the suite. Logie and Sam snuggled together on the two-seater, Lin curled into a matching armchair, and Harry draped his legs over the arm of another while Riley sprawled on the floor, her back against Harry's chair.

There was a tap on the door and Benedict opened it, looking in as Riley scrambled to her feet.

"I see you're settling in," he said. "Everything okay?"

"Yes, thanks. My housemates—ex-housemates— have been helping me move."

Benedict nodded politely. "Well, if you have all you need, I'll leave you with your friends."

"Have some coffee with us?" she suggested.

"Thanks," he said, "but I'll pour myself one to take back to my study."

After waving off her friends later, Riley returned

by a side path to the back of the house. Passing the lighted window of Benedict's office, she could see him using a portable computer at his desk.

In the kitchen there was still half a jug of coffee in the machine. Picking it up, she went along the passageway and tapped on the office door.

Benedict called, "Yes?"

Riley opened the door. "I wondered if you'd like a refill. You don't take sugar and milk, do you?" He hadn't added any the night of the dinner party.

"Thanks." He pushed his empty cup toward her. "But you don't need to stay up to wait on me. That's not part of the job."

"What about breakfast?"

"I have it at a café in my office building. In the mornings I generally go for a run first thing and have a juice or a cup of coffee afterward, but I can fix that myself. The only meal you need to cook regularly is dinner, and sometimes I'm not here for that. On weekends I can fend for myself if I'm here and don't have guests." He fished a document out of a drawer. "Here's your contract. Read it over."

It was only a single sheet, and she couldn't fault it. "It looks fine," she told him.

He handed her a pen and she wrote her name at the foot of the page, repeated the procedure on a copy.

While he did the same, Riley asked, "The telephone in my room—is it an extension?"

"You have your own line. You pay for long-distance calls but I take care of the line rent."

"Oh…thank you."

"It's simpler that way," he said dismissively, handing her one of the copies.

She supposed he didn't want to be answering calls

for his housekeeper. "Um...do I take messages for you?"

"No need. When I'm at the office or don't want to be disturbed I switch on the answering machine." He picked up his coffee, glancing at the screen in front of him. "Anything else you need to know?"

He said it quite pleasantly, but Riley gathered he was dismissing her. "Not tonight," she said. "There probably will be things..."

"Just ask as they arise."

"Good night, then."

"Good night, Riley. I'm glad you're here."

She went out feeling ridiculously warmed and glowing.

The following evening Riley served Benedict and his guests juicy, tender steaks, new potatoes drenched in minted butter, a selection of fresh market vegetables, and a dessert of spicy apple pie with cream.

She was washing up when Benedict came into the kitchen, holding a liqueur glass in one hand and a bottle in the other. "My visitors send compliments on the meal, Riley."

"It wasn't anything fancy—I thought I'd better play safe until I've got used to the stove. I hope you didn't mind."

"It was superb. Would you like a drink?" He held up the bottle and the empty glass.

She guessed it was some kind of reward. "Thanks, I will." As he poured it for her, she asked, "Shall I tidy up in there after you've finished?"

"No. We could be talking for hours. I hope to sign an agreement with the guy by the end of the week." He grinned at her, handing over the glass. "Thanks to you, he's in a nicely mellow mood. You go to bed if you want to. And you don't need to get up early. I'll see you when I get home from work tomorrow.''

When he did come home on Thursday he found her carefully separating some schnitzels she'd found in the freezer. ''Everything okay?'' he asked.

''Fine. What time do you want dinner?''

''Anytime. Could you bring a tray to my study? I've got work to catch up on.''

When she took the tray in later he scarcely looked up as he thanked her.

''There's some apple pie left from last night,'' she told him. ''I could heat it for you, or would you rather have something else?''

''I'll have the pie. Don't bother heating it.''

But the next evening he said, ''I'll eat in the kitchen—and would you join me? Unless you'd prefer to have yours alone?''

She didn't, and they both ate at the kitchen table. Benedict opened a bottle of wine and poured two glasses. ''I got my new contract signed this morning.''

''The man who was here the other night?''

''Right.'' He put down the bottle, raised his glass and waited for her to do the same. ''To good food and its effect on business.''

Riley grinned, lifting her own glass. ''And I believe you plied him with drink too. Do you think that might have had something to do with it?''

Benedict was sipping his wine. He put down the glass. ''We had a few glasses of wine with dinner and a liqueur afterward. He was still compos mentis.''

''But well oiled.'' She slanted him a mischievous look. ''And *very* mellow.''

He laughed. "He didn't sign until this morning," he reminded her. "In the bright light of day. My conscience is clear."

"Do businessmen have consciences?"

He looked at her coolly. "I'm not the only one who jumps to conclusions, am I?"

Riley's tongue nervously examined her slightly imperfect tooth. "You're right, I shouldn't buy in to stereotypes. I'm sure you're as pure as the driven snow."

His eyebrows lifted. "You are?" In his eyes something gleamed—curiosity, perhaps. Or something else. Maybe he just couldn't help looking at a woman that way—with an undercurrent of sexuality.

"In business, I mean," Riley said hastily.

"But you're not so sure about other areas of my life?" His expression turned quizzical.

"I didn't say that."

"Implied it."

"It wasn't meant to imply anything. What you do with your life is nothing to do with me." She put down her glass and picked up her knife and fork to attack the lamb chop on her plate. "I've given my notice at the day care center. After next week I'm all yours—I mean, um…"

Benedict laughed, but mercifully didn't take up her faux pas. "Will you miss it?"

He still wasn't sure she could stand being alone, she guessed. "I'll be fine." She'd have more quiet time to study. "And if I want company I have lots of friends I can visit or go out with."

Benedict was easy to work for. He didn't leave his clothes lying about, although Riley did find a stray sock one morning on the floor of his bathroom, and on another occasion when she was vacuuming she fished out a pair of shoes from under a sofa. His desk was sometimes covered with folders and papers, but she didn't dare touch them.

He was a neat sleeper too. His bed was hardly rumpled in the mornings, and there was never any evidence that he'd shared it with anyone.

Although she wasn't really a morning person, most days she hauled herself out of bed and dressed before Benedict came in from his morning run, and switched on the coffee machine for him.

She learned that Benedict liked his coffee hot and strong, his steak juicy but not mooing, and he didn't like brussels sprouts at all.

Sunday and Tuesday were her usual free days, and she gathered he generally ate out. The third Tuesday after she'd moved in, he arrived home about nine-thirty as she was seeing off Harry and Logie, after spending a couple of hours lounging around her suite with coffee, coke and beer, listening to pop music.

Next morning Benedict asked Riley to drive him to work. "I have a breakfast meeting," he told her. "I'd like to go through some notes beforehand."

"Okay," she said, but when they went to the garage and he swung toward the BMW, she was startled. "You want me to drive that?"

Benedict paused. "Why not?"

"I didn't think you'd trust me."

"Of course I trust you, Riley. But if you'd feel more comfortable with your own car, we'll take that."

"I'm not used to an automatic gear shift." Or to a

luxury car that must have cost a mind-boggling amount of money.

Benedict shrugged and changed direction. "I'll take you for a test drive soon and get you accustomed to it."

He did so that evening, shortly after he got home, backing the car out of the garage himself but then putting her into the driver's seat.

Slipping in beside her, he laughed. "You'll need to adjust the seat."

"I know." The foot pedals seemed miles away and she could scarcely see over the steering wheel. "How do I do it?"

He leaned over and did it for her, bringing the seat up and forward. His hair briefly brushed her cheek, surprising her with its warmth and silky texture. Surreptitiously she breathed in the wood-spice fragrance of his aftershave or whatever it was that he used.

Then he was straightening. "Better?"

"Thanks." Her hands tightened on the cold curve of the steering wheel. Fervently she hoped he had no idea of the effect he had on her.

He's your boss, she reminded herself sternly. You're only the housekeeper-chauffeur, and don't forget it.

Chapter Five

Benedict cleared his throat. "Ready?"

Staring through the windscreen, Riley answered, "Yes."

"There's no need to be nervous," he told her. "It's very easy to drive."

The car was a positive dream. Following Benedict's instructions and street directions, eventually she drew up on the grass verge of a quiet little bay. A few shaggy-barked pohutukawa trees bowed over the sand, and water lapped at the narrow strip of beach. The road followed the curve of the shoreline, and the other side was lined with houses.

Several children and a dun-colored dog ran in and out of the shallow waves that were turning from blue-green to a metallic gray sheen, and a single timid star hung in the sky.

"Feel like stretching your legs?" Benedict asked.

It looked nice out there—cool and still. "Yes."

She locked the car and handed him the keys as they

turned to stroll along the grass parallel with the beach. One of the children threw a stick into the water, and the dog plunged after it, raising a halo of spray. Distracted, Riley tripped on a small rock poking up through the grass, and Benedict's hand closed about her arm, steadying her. "Careful."

"Thanks," she said. "I should watch where I put my feet."

He didn't reply, but his hand stayed cupping her elbow. Sort of old-fashioned, but Riley found she liked it. Perhaps too damn much.

They walked to where the road left the bay and a jutting headland thrust seaward, with several large houses arrogantly perched on its flat top. A couple of lights winked on behind distant windows even though it wasn't really dark yet.

Riley turned toward the sea view, slipping from Benedict's hold. She shoved her hands into the pockets of her jeans. "Shall we go back along the sand?"

"If you'd like to."

He went down the slight slope to where the grass abruptly stopped at the top of a low bank, and offered her his hand. But Riley had already shed her shoes and was jumping lightly down beside him.

The sand was soft and pale, studded with shell fragments. The dog, pursued by the children, ran toward them, its coat wet and shiny. It outstripped its young companions and loped up to Riley and Benedict, skipping about them.

One of the children called, "*Here,* boy!"

The dog stopped, looked, and then shook itself vigorously. Cold, salty droplets fell on Riley's hair and face and soaked her thin T-shirt, and she gave a small

squawk, instinctively lifting her hands and step-
ping back.

Benedict said something short and sharp, and Riley
wiped her eyes and opened them to see the children
running up, panting. The eldest, a boy of about
twelve, gasped, "Sorry!" He gripped the dog's collar.
"Bad dog!" he admonished.

"Shouldn't that animal be on a leash?" Benedict
asked sternly. There were damp patches on his shirt
too, but he wasn't as thoroughly wet as Riley.

The boy looked guilty but defensive. "He needs to
run sometimes."

"Never mind," Riley said, laughing. "It'll soon
dry." She tugged at Benedict's arm. "No harm
done."

Benedict looked down at her and she dropped her
hand. His eyes glittered, but he followed as she turned
to walk on. The children and the dog were scrambling
to the grass verge, jostling each other as they checked
for oncoming cars before crossing the road.

"You don't need to be angry," Riley said. Her
shirt felt clammy. She pulled the fabric away from
her body and tried ineffectually to shake out some of
the dampness.

"I'm not angry."

"Annoyed, then."

"What makes you think I'm annoyed?"

"The way you looked at me just now. As if it was
my fault."

Patiently he said, "I know it wasn't your fault. You
were mistaken."

"Was I?" Riley said encouragingly.

Benedict laughed in a slightly exasperated way.
"How do you expect a man to react when you look

as though you're a candidate in a wet T-shirt contest?''

''What?'' Startled, she glanced down at herself and saw all too plainly what he meant. ''Oh, sh-shoot!'' Raising her eyes again, she blurted out, ''But you're not—I mean, you're my employer!''

''I also happen to be a man.''

''I'm your housekeeper!'' She probably sounded shocked. In a way she was. She'd known from the start that she would have to keep a rein on her attraction to Benedict Falkner, and he'd clearly indicated that he saw her as domestic help, nothing else. She'd been confident that unreciprocated lust wouldn't lead to emotional complications. Mutual lust was something totally different. Thrilling, surprising...and potentially disastrous.

Benedict was laughing again, softly. ''I know,'' he said, with a disconcerting glint in the depths of his eyes. ''Only, Mrs. Hardy never looked like you do now.''

She shouldn't be feeling pleased. It was flattering that he'd admitted she could turn him on, but that was only because his male hormones were reacting to a purely physical phenomenon. It didn't mean that he intended to carry it any further. And if he did, he'd probably regret compromising their employer-employee relationship.

So would she, Riley reminded herself. Of course she would. ''What about Tiffany?'' she demanded. Tiffany would have looked terrific in sackcloth, let alone a wet T-shirt.

''Tiffany?'' Benedict's expression changed so suddenly she might have slapped him. Had he forgotten about Tiffany?

Impossible.

"You said you wanted her for your girlfriend."
She was reminding herself as much as him.

"Did I say that?" Benedict murmured, frowning.

"Sort of. You did…you *do* still want her, don't
you? I mean—" Riley swallowed and went on
bravely "—she's beautiful, and nice, and you seem
very…very suited to each other."

"Do we?" He looked at her thoughtfully. They had
almost reached the place where she'd parked the car,
and he veered across the sand toward it.

"Yes." Trailing a little behind him, Riley tried to
sound positive.

"Do you think I'd measure up?"

Riley blinked up at him. The shadows cast by one
of the pohutukawas softened his expression, but she
couldn't read his eyes in the growing gloom. "You
mean are you good enough for her?"

"I suppose," he said slowly, "that is what I
mean."

"Of course you are!" Heavens, any woman in her
right mind would jump at him. Any woman who
wasn't his housekeeper, with too much to lose from
a messy affair that would probably cost her the best
job she'd ever had. Plus a badly bruised heart. "And
she likes you."

"Likes?" He didn't seem exactly impressed.

"She asked me for the recipe of that dessert I
made."

His head tilted. "What?" Obviously he didn't follow her reasoning.

"You had two helpings, she told me," Riley explained. "And then she asked me for the recipe."

"And that proves something?"

"No, not exactly, but…" She fought for the words. "It might *indicate* something. Don't you think?"

"It might, I suppose." He moved abruptly, opening the car door. "Are you game to drive us back?"

"All right." Riley brushed past him and took the driver's seat.

When she'd started the engine, he suggested, "Why don't we stop on the way and buy a take-away meal? You won't want to start cooking when we get home."

"I don't mind cooking, but if you feel like fish and chips or something…?"

"Chinese," he said. "Do you like Chinese?"

"Yes, I do."

"Good. I know a place that makes the best wontons."

He told her where to pull up, and on his instructions she stayed in the car until he came back with four bags giving off mouthwatering smells.

A few minutes later she drove into the garage, and the automatic doors closed almost silently behind them.

When they'd got out of the car she gave him the keys. "Thanks for the lesson. Can I carry some of those?" She eyed the bags cradled on one of his arms.

He gave her a quizzical look. "No." As if it was funny she'd even offered.

She opened the door into the house for him, then locked it behind them.

Benedict nodded his thanks. "Will you feel confident about driving my car now?"

"I don't know about confident, but I'll be all right with a bit more experience."

"Maybe you should drive me to and from work for a week or so, just for practice."

"If you like," she agreed as they headed for the kitchen. "Do you want to take a plate to your study or eat here?" she asked, pushing open the doors.

"Here," he answered, placing the bags on the table. "White wine?"

"Sounds good." Riley was already reaching for plates.

She pulled plastic foam containers from the bags and piled food on the plates while he poured the wine, and they ate with forks and fingers. "The only way to eat wontons," Riley decreed, picking up one of the crisp, delicate envelopes and crunching into it. "Mmm, you're right. This is *great*."

Winding her ankles about the legs of her chair, she parked her elbows on the table and dug her fork into the chow mein.

The big kitchen was warm, and Riley's shirt had nearly dried, but a faint odor of seawater still hung about her. After swallowing a mouthful of noodles and vegetables she said, "Don't you like dogs?"

"Haven't had much to do with them. I always wanted a dog when I was a kid."

"You never had one?"

"Nope."

"Shame. It's a boy thing, isn't it? I suppose your parents didn't want a dog around."

"My parents didn't even want *me* around."

Her shocked gaze swept up to meet his.

Benedict looked back at her and gave a short laugh. "That wasn't a bid for sympathy, just a simple statement of fact. Forget it." He bent his head and shoved a forkful of food into his mouth.

"Why?" she asked.

His glance seemed impatient. He picked up his wine and drank some. "You don't want to know the story of my life."

"Isn't it an interesting story?"

He applied himself to his meal again, his face closed. "It's very boring."

Riley doubted that. "I was right about you," she mused.

"In what way?" His eyes narrowed watchfully.

"At first sight—at least, once I got a good look at you—I sort of assumed you'd been born wealthy."

"Wrong."

"That was my second thought." She was curious now. "That maybe you weren't born into money, but you'd acquired it somehow...."

"I worked for it," he said shortly.

"So you said. I wasn't suggesting otherwise." He must have worked damned hard. She knew he still did. "What made you think your parents didn't want you?" she asked him, her voice soft.

"Could be the fact that they threw me out when I was sixteen," he said cynically.

Riley was speechless. She'd heard of such things, but it still seemed inconceivable that parents could do that. "That's awful," she said at last, knowing how inadequate a remark it was. "I'm so sorry."

A flicker of surprise crossed his face, to be replaced by an even deeper cynicism. "It was the best thing they ever did for me."

"Really?"

"You don't believe that," he said. "Let me guess, you come from a large, loving family." He almost made it sound like a sin. "You probably still spend

Christmas at home with your parents. Or are they in the States?"

"Yes, they are, and I miss them." She'd spent last Christmas with her eldest brother who had returned to New Zealand and now farmed in the Waikato district to the south. Benedict's accuracy—or the derisive tone he'd used—made her defensive, but she wasn't going to deny that she was fond of her family. "Are you jealous?" she challenged, looking straight at him.

His jaw clenched, and a spark of anger lit his eyes. Then he sat back, his gaze sweeping down to his wine before he picked up the glass and swallowed some. "How did you guess?" he drawled, replacing the glass. His tone hadn't altered, but somehow the mockery had lost its sting.

"How did *you* guess about my family?" she asked.

Benedict smiled in a slightly mocking way. "Easily," he scoffed. "You have that innocent air of confidence that comes with being loved and secure. You get on with people in groups—your references bear that out—but you're well able to stick up for yourself when threatened. Or when you *think* you're being threatened. I'd say you had at least a couple of brothers...probably older than you, and...any sisters?"

"Three brothers," she grudgingly allowed. "No sisters. Did you ever think of taking up fortune-telling?"

Benedict's grin dispelled any hint of temper. "It's simple observation. There's nothing supernatural about it."

"Impressive," she told him. "Some party trick."

He shook his head, spearing a morsel of pork that was dripping with sauce and lifting it from his plate.

"Not a party trick. More of a business skill that I've developed."

Reading people? She'd have to watch herself around this man. He was positively scary. "A business skill?" she queried.

He shrugged. "Choosing the right people to work for—and later to work for me—has been important. And sound judgment based on instinct and experience is more useful than any number of references."

He hadn't been terribly interested in hers, not even asking for them until she brought the subject up. "Where was your instinct and judgment the day I scratched your car?" she demanded, hoping to score a point. "You thought I was running away."

"At first," he acknowledged. "What else was I to think when you were spitting and scratching—and biting…" The gleam of laughter in his eyes acknowledged that he knew she wouldn't like being reminded of that yet again. "…like a cornered kitten?"

Revolted, she said, "I am not a *kitten!* I didn't spit or scratch—and if you hadn't grabbed me like some car park mugger I wouldn't have needed to…to scream, either."

He laughed outright. "You certainly have a healthy pair of lungs. I thought those two guys were going to beat me up first and ask questions later."

"Except you got in with that fast mouth of yours and talked them out of it. A great example of male solidarity," Riley said waspishly. "In two seconds flat you had them on your side. So much for gallantry."

"It was an example of male impartiality in the face of facts, and our innate sense of fair play. You *had* damaged my car and been caught red-handed. Any

reasonable man would have seen that I was the injured party.''

Knowing he expected her to rise to the bait, but
unable to ignore it, Riley launched into attack mode,
the light of battle in her eyes. ''And I suppose any
reasonable man would have jumped to the same unreasonable conclusion that you did!'' she said with
withering sarcasm. ''That's male logic for you!''

''The evidence suggested—''

''Huh!''

They argued the age-old male/female dichotomy
with energy and enthusiasm, thoroughly enjoying
themselves, and even squabbled amicably about who
should have the last wonton.

''You eat it,'' Riley said. ''I've had my share.''

''I've eaten twice as much as you.''

''You need it, you're bigger than me.''

''Everyone's bigger than you.'' He grinned as his
eyes slipped over what he could see of her.

Riley made a face at him. ''That's mean.''

Benedict abruptly sobered. ''Does it bother you? I
didn't mean to hurt your feelings, Riley. As one who
spent the major part of my high school years being
called Shortz—''

The telephone on the wall shrilled.

Benedict got up quickly. ''I haven't switched off
the answer machine.'' He snatched the receiver from
the hook before the machine could cut in. ''Hello?
Oh, Tiffany…no, it's not inconvenient at all.''

Riley stood up and removed her empty plate from
the table. Benedict motioned to her to take his too,
although there were still a couple of bits of pork and
some noodles on it.

She finished clearing up, trying to ignore the conversation in the background. Not that she could glean much from Benedict's end of it—Tiffany seemed to be doing most of the talking—but he was in no hurry to terminate the call.

When the plates were in the washer she turned to him and whispered, "Shall I go?"

He shook his head, put his palm over the mouthpiece and said, "Won't be long."

Riley wiped the table and rinsed out the sponge with a noisy rush of water, then washed and dried the wineglasses. Benedict was still on the phone when she passed him to replace the glasses in their cabinet in the dining room.

She slammed the cabinet door on them and went back to the kitchen, entering as Benedict put the receiver down at last.

"That was Tiffany," he said, unnecessarily. "She's having a birthday party."

And he was invited, obviously. "That's nice. When?"

"Saturday week."

"So you won't be wanting dinner that night?"

"You think I should go?"

"Of course you should go!" She wasn't sure why he was looking at her that way, as if her opinion mattered.

"She asked if I wanted to bring a partner."

Riley's throat felt tight. "That means she doesn't want you to."

"Does it?"

What had happened to his vaunted people-reading skills? "Of course!" she said crossly. "Otherwise she'd just have said to bring someone."

It was rather touching that a man as successful and

self-confident as Benedict Falkner could be so diffi-
dent with a woman who was sending him all the right
signals.

His eyes glazed as if he were looking at something
else, not Riley. Maybe he couldn't believe his luck.
He'd more or less said that he didn't feel he was good
enough for Tiffany, hadn't he?

He must be in love with her. Only love could make
him so unsure of himself, Riley concluded, ignoring
the way her chest wall seemed to be squeezing her
heart. "You can't turn up with someone else," she
told him earnestly.

He focused on her again. "You don't think that
stirring up a bit of jealousy could be, um, useful?"

About to veto the idea outright, Riley paused. "I
don't know her well enough to say," she decided.
"And I wasn't hired to give you advice on your love
life." Suddenly she had developed a distaste for this
conversation. "You're the one who's so slick at fig-
uring people out."

He frowned at her as though he was seeing something else, or looking right through her. "Some people are more complex than others."

He'd pinpointed Riley's background with uncanny
accuracy, and she wouldn't have thought that Tiffany
was a particularly complex person. However, as she'd
just told Benedict, she was hardly qualified to give an
opinion. Presumably the blue, blue eyes, bright blond
hair and sunny manner held hidden depths.

She swallowed hard. "Have you invited her out?"
she demanded, already reneging on her resolve not to
advise him.

"Not on a one-to-one basis."

Surely he wasn't shy? Riley regarded him with a

candid stare. "Well, what are you waiting for?" she asked aggressively. "Tiffany's everything you want, isn't she?"

He stared back at her, taking an age to answer. "Yes," he said at last. "She's everything I've ever wanted in a woman."

All his dreams come true. She could believe that. Tiffany was any man's dream woman. And it wasn't every man who could win a woman like that, but Benedict wasn't just any man. "So go for it," she said. "Let her know you're interested."

"Is that what you'd do?" he enquired, his eyes oddly alert and curious. "Supposing you were interested in a man?"

"Of course." Well, any man except him. Any man she had a chance with...and wasn't working for. "But Tiffany's probably different." Apart from her privileged upbringing, which very likely included traditional male-female social standards, Tiffany's natural beauty would have allowed her to wait for a man to make the first move. "She wouldn't say it outright, but she's given you your cue. Now it's up to you. Go to the party, and ask her out."

His brows drew together. "You really think she's expecting that?"

"I'm sure she is!"

"And that's what you think I should do?" he pressed.

"Yes!" She glared at him. "I just *told* you that." So why did she have the feeling that a whole flotilla of boats was going up in flames behind her? "Don't be a wuss!" Although it was difficult to imagine him being anything of the kind.

Maybe he was offended. Thrusting his hands into

his pockets, he rocked back slightly on his heels, and his mouth tightened. "Thanks for the suggestion. I'll take it up."

Then he said good-night and brusquely strode past her and out of the kitchen.

"Damn!" Riley muttered for no reason in particular. A discarded food container had somehow escaped and lay under the table, looking disgusting. She scooped it up and crushed it in her hands with a gratifying crackle before lifting the lid of the bin and thrusting the container inside.

It would have been much more satisfying to throw it.

Chapter Six

The weekend of Tiffany's party Benedict told Riley to have Saturday off as well as Sunday, and she took the opportunity to drive south and visit her brother, arriving back late on Sunday to an empty garage and a quiet house. She tried not to think about where Benedict might be spending the night.

She didn't hear his car before she went to sleep, but next morning she was spreading marmalade on a piece of toast at the kitchen counter when he came in, dressed in running shoes, athlete's shorts and a T-shirt. He didn't seem out of breath after his run, but he wiped the back of his hand over a faint shine on his brow as he crossed the room.

"Good morning," he said. "Any coffee going?"

"Nearly ready." She indicated the machine, still bubbling, and he grabbed a coffee mug and waited.

Riley bit into her toast, chewed briefly and swallowed. "How was the party?" she asked nonchalantly.

Benedict gave her a short, searching look. "Very enjoyable, thank you."

"Have you, um, did you...?"

He leaned back against the counter, looking at her with peculiar intensity. "I invited Tiffany to have dinner with me."

Riley injected a false enthusiasm into her voice. "Oh, good! Where are you taking her?"

"You're assuming she said yes?"

"She did, didn't she?" Riley's emotions were torn. The baser ones couldn't help hoping Tiffany had said no. But then Benedict would have been hurt, and it would be Riley's fault for encouraging him to make a move.

"She did," Benedict confirmed. "I haven't decided where to go. Do you have any suggestions? If I bring her here—"

"No!"

His brows lifted in enquiry. "No?"

"For a first date," Riley said hastily, "you should take her somewhere special—a really good restaurant, maybe a show or something, as well. You don't want to look cheap, do you?"

His eyes gleamed. "I'd hate to look cheap. I'll book a table at a restaurant. Thanks for the tip."

Riley's tongue worried at her tooth, and she looked at him suspiciously. "You don't need my advice," she guessed shrewdly. "I'm sure you're not that inexperienced." So why was he stringing her along?

Perhaps he had a warped sense of humor. It wouldn't be the first time she'd suspected him of enjoying some private joke at her expense. "Are you laughing at me?" she demanded.

"Certainly not. I'm grateful. You see, Tiffany

is...well, she's different from most of the women I've dated.''

The hollow feeling that was becoming unnervingly familiar returned. ''Why?'' she asked baldly.

His answer was unexpected. ''I told you,'' he said, ''I decided as a teenager that I was going to be rich.'' His mouth twisted. ''I guess you think that's a shallow ambition.''

Possibly it was, but she wasn't judging him. What he called ambition might have disguised a deeper need for security after a disturbed childhood. ''Most people would like to be rich,'' she said, ''but not many actually achieve it by their own efforts. I respect that.''

The coffee machine stopped bubbling, and he paused to fill his mug. Turning again, he stared down at the dark depths. ''I've achieved most things I set out to do. I'm thirty-two years old, and I built this place with the idea that pretty soon I'd have a wife and family to share it with.''

Riley swallowed. ''That's a natural hope.''

He looked up. ''I'd always thought I'd marry someone like Tiffany, someone with a background.''

She remembered that when she'd first seen this house she'd been reminded of a fairy-tale castle. Maybe as a boy he'd read fairy stories and dreamed of marrying a princess. ''Everyone has a background,'' she reminded him. ''You mean someone with money and class. You want your marriage to reflect your upwardly mobile lifestyle.''

She thought his taut cheeks became tinged with color. ''To put it crudely,'' he agreed curtly. ''In my defense, I'm not interested in her money or her father's money. I have enough of my own. But you said yourself, Tiffany's perfect.''

"She is," Riley concurred flatly. "And she's nice. Too nice to be married to someone who doesn't love her."

"You've misunderstood." His voice was cold. "I wouldn't ask any woman to marry me if I didn't love her."

"Oh. Then you have nothing to worry about, do you?"

After a moment he said, "She might not love me."

"How long have you known her?"

He shrugged. "A couple of months."

She'd thought it must be longer. He'd known Riley for nearly as long as that.

"How did you meet her?"

He didn't answer immediately. "Her father and I have done business together. I invited him to bring his family along to a barbecue here, and Tiffany insisted on helping out, carrying food from the kitchen and clearing up afterward. Mrs. Hardy was very taken with her."

"And you were too."

He glanced at her. "I saw she'd be easy to love."

"Why didn't you ask her out, back then?"

He shrugged. "Several reasons. I thought maybe I was too old for her—"

"How old is she?" Riley tried hard to concentrate on the relevant issues.

"Twenty-three, now. It seems older than twenty-two," he said wryly.

"Nine years isn't so much." Eight was even less.

"Maybe it depends on what you—*I* did in those years."

"Like amassing a fortune?" It was hardly a drawback in the matrimonial stakes.

"Like spending time in Borstal," Benedict said bluntly. "Among other things."

"Reform school?" Riley nearly choked on her toast. "That must have been a long time ago." Borstal was supposed to rehabilitate underage offenders, wasn't it? And Benedict certainly looked thoroughly rehabilitated to her.

"What had you done?"

"Gone about the quickest way of getting rich, as I thought then. Got into a teenage gang that tried to rob a bank."

A bank robber? *Benedict?* "With guns?" she asked, feeling queasy.

"I had a fake one—a toy gun. I was fifteen and stupid. One of the guys had a real one, although I didn't know that until he pulled it out and started waving it at the tellers. In a way I think I didn't believe any of it was real—just a boys' fantasy. Fortunately we got caught—"

"Fortunately?"

"The police and the courts made it very obvious that it was no fantasy," he said grimly. "The whole experience was pretty scary. If we'd got away with it I might just have been dumb enough to think crime was a viable way of life. My old man did. But of course like any adolescent I thought that I was smarter than he was and wouldn't get caught."

Her eyes widened. "Your father was a criminal?"

"He spent most of his life in and out of jail for small crimes. Now he's in a retirement home. A bit early, but he wants for nothing and has no more excuses for dishonesty."

"Are you paying for his keep?"

Benedict's eyelids flickered upward. "I don't want him in jail again—the media would make a meal of it."

Meaning he was protecting his own reputation. She wondered if that was all it was. "What about your mother?"

"My mother died of alcohol poisoning when I was twenty-one. I didn't go to the funeral."

Shock silenced her. After a second she said, "Why did they throw you out?" She hadn't dared ask before, but now he seemed to be in a confiding mood. If his father was a petty thief and his mother had been an alcoholic, it couldn't have been moral indignation, surely?

Benedict gave a twisted smile. "While I was locked up, I turned my life around, thanks to a couple of good, tough men on the staff. I learned from their example that honesty and…honor…had to be fought for and were hard to sustain, not sissy qualities to despise and take advantage of. I guess when I came out of there I was insufferably self-righteous, convinced I could reform my parents and turn us into a real family. I don't blame them for telling me to bug off."

Riley did. Maybe being shown the right road by a teenager—and their own son—had been a bit much to swallow, but surely they could have tried to turn themselves around for his sake? "It must have been awful being on your own at that age."

"I wasn't quite on my own. My friend the chaplain arranged accommodation and put me in touch with some useful people. I was lucky."

Yet he must have made tremendous efforts to develop not only his business, but his sophisticated image, to break out of the mold he'd been cast in. He'd focused on a dream and set out to fulfill it.

And part of the dream was a home like this, with a suitable, classy, loving wife to grace it, and children who wouldn't have to suffer the deprivations that had bedeviled his own childhood.

That wasn't an unworthy ambition. Lots of men in his position would have happily spent their money on transient pleasures and taken willing women to their beds without any intention of commitment. Benedict was different. He wanted more than that. And he'd struggled against tremendous odds to fulfill his dreams.

He picked up his coffee cup and drained it. "Anyway, I didn't mean to tell you the story of my life. You're too easy to talk to, Riley."

She'd been told that before. Her housemates used to pour out their troubles to her when one of their relationships hit a rocky patch. Even her brothers had sometimes enlisted her help before divulging some peccadillo to their parents.

He took his cup to the sink, and Riley said, "I'll deal with that."

"Thanks." He nodded to her and went swiftly from the room. She had the impression he was embarrassed about having told her so much.

Having taken Saturday off, Riley dropped Benedict at work on Tuesday. He paused as he was getting out and said, "Could you pick me up later tonight at Glen Innes? I'll get a cab out there from the office. Nine o'clock. I'll give you the address."

It was a gymnasium. She supposed he used it to

maintain his nice male body in top order. But when she got there she didn't at first see him. A group of teenage boys was hanging about in the darkness outside the big, unlit building, most of them in baggy track pants and bulky sports shoes. There seemed to be a bit of pushing and shoving going on, and she wasn't sure if they were just larking about or gearing up to a genuine fight.

Then the group parted momentarily and she saw Benedict's familiar broad-shouldered figure in the middle of them, just as one young man, at least a head taller than he was, laid a large hand on his shoulder.

Riley was out of the car and across the pavement before she'd even thought about it. Her hands curling into fists, she yelled, "Leave him alone!"

Several heads turned, and then Benedict was walking toward her. "Riley," he said. "Come and meet my team."

Team? These yobs?

He drew her toward them. "This is Dak, Pene, Bubs, Mad Max…"

Some of them mumbled, "Hi" and others stepped forward to shake her hand.

"Hey, Coach, she your girl?" asked a chunky brown-skinned boy with a cheeky grin, and a ponytail peeping from his knitted beanie hat.

"She's my housekeeper," Benedict told them.

A chorus of hoots and whistles greeted that, and Benedict, hardly raising his voice, said, "Cool it, guys."

Amazingly they did. At least half of them were bigger than Benedict, but the note of authority in his casual words had them shuffling and muttering apol-

ogies to Riley like the overgrown schoolboys she realized they were.

"See you all next week," Benedict said, and
steered Riley back to the car.

When she'd started the engine he said, "Were you
planning to rescue me?"

He was laughing at her. "They looked like…"

"Thugs? They're just a bunch of kids who need
something to keep them occupied, something to aim
for."

Like the kid he'd once been. "I suppose you think
I was pretty stupid."

"I think you were pretty courageous," Benedict
argued. "Stupid, too," he conceded with a judicial
air. "But I'm touched at you coming to my defense."

"What are you coaching them in?"

"Basketball."

She'd have imagined boxing, maybe. But basketball? "Did you ever play?"

"I got suckered into it. The sports coach at the
Borstal training school asked me what I'd like to play
and I said basketball, thinking that'd be the end of it.
He took me up on it, and I told him he was nuts, I'd
be no good on the court. Then he said that with that
attitude I'd be a loser all my life and walked away in
disgust." Benedict gave a crack of laughter. "He was
some psychologist. I decided to show him, and for
my size I wasn't bad, but I was never going to be tall
enough to be a champion. Then a few years back I
read about this program and volunteered to coach. I'm
probably projecting onto them," he said carelessly.
"Not that my boys are world champions. But they
enjoy it and it keeps them off the streets at least one
night a week."

"I think it's great," Riley said softly. It gave her an interesting new slant on his character. "My boys" he'd called them, as though he was quite proud of them. Maybe even fond of them. He'd be a good father some day.

Benedict made a scoffing sound. "I owe some people I'll never be able to repay. The only thing I can do is try to pass on a fraction of what they gave me. Besides, I enjoy it."

On Wednesday morning Benedict said he wouldn't be needing dinner that night.

He was taking Tiffany out, of course. Riley gave him a bright smile and said, "Have a good time."

"Thank you." Maybe there was irony in his voice. Or maybe she'd imagined it. She was sure he was over the moon that Tiffany had agreed to go on a date with him.

The next day Riley deliberately waited until she'd heard him leave before she entered the kitchen. She couldn't bear to ask how his evening had been. And she was relieved that when he came home he didn't volunteer to tell her.

Benedict was often out in the evening. One time he mentioned that his "boys" were playing in a tournament all day Saturday and he planned to take them out for a meal afterward. "You can have the night off," he said.

"Can I come and watch?" she asked impulsively. She knew how much the team meant to him. She'd learned the names of the boys now and enjoyed hearing about them. A couple of them had scrapes with the law, and she suspected that along with basketball, Benedict coached them in life skills.

"Sure," he said. "If you're interested. They can do with some cheering on."

"I'll bring some friends," she said, and was as good as her word. She arrived with a group that included her ex-housemates, provided them with ribbons, makeshift flags and face paint in the team's colors, and led the cheering herself.

The boys made it through to the finals against all expectations and were only beaten at the end. It was good enough, and they hoisted the coach to their shoulders and bore him off the court. Riley had never seen Benedict look so happy.

He bounded up the tiers of seats to her and said, "Thanks for the encouragement—to all of you!" he added, taking in her friends. "The boys would like you to join us for a meal."

Most of them had other things arranged, but Riley and Harry accepted and enjoyed a somewhat riotous evening at the pizza parlor the team had chosen, although Benedict had offered a more upmarket venue.

Afterward Benedict drove some of the boys home and he didn't come back to the house until after Riley was in bed, but the next day he thanked her again. "The boys really appreciated it," he said. "A lot of their parents aren't interested, you know."

"What about Tiffany?"

He blinked. "Tiffany? I don't think she'd fit in that...atmosphere, do you?"

"I think she'd try." He obviously thought of the girl as a princess in her ivory tower. Admittedly it was difficult to imagine her painting her face red and green and yelling encouragement from the sidelines, but surely she'd take an interest for Benedict's sake.

Benedict shook his head. "She's not really sports minded. She likes ballet and opera."

The two weren't mutually exclusive, she wanted to tell him, but he knew Tiffany better than she did.

A few days later Benedict brought a group of people for a late supper—Tiffany among them. They invaded the kitchen as Riley was about to undress for bed, and after a small hesitation she opened the door of her suite and went to see if she was wanted.

Benedict introduced his friends. "And you know Tiffany."

Tiffany seemed pleased to see her again. "Hello! Benedict said he'd hired you to take Mrs. Hardy's place. Are you enjoying the job?"

"Very much," Riley answered politely. Obviously, Tiffany wasn't a bit worried about another woman living in the same house as Benedict. Not if the other woman was Riley, anyway. "Would you like me to make you some supper?" she asked him.

"Does he keep you working all night?" Tiffany sent him a teasing smile, and a couple of the others laughed. "What a slave driver!"

Riley answered, "Not at all. He's very considerate. What would you like to eat?" she asked Benedict.

"Thanks for the offer, but that would be above and beyond, Riley," Benedict said. "We're just having coffee."

"We can manage," Tiffany told her breezily. "There's no need to keep you up."

"Join us if you like," Benedict invited her, and Riley saw the surprised look Tiffany gave him. He'd probably given away his lower-class origins by suggesting that the housekeeper share their supper.

"Thank you, Mr. Falkner," Riley said primly,

drawing a surprised look of his own to her. "But I was just going to bed."

Long after she'd closed her bedroom door she could hear them laughing and talking in the kitchen. Evidently they'd decided to have their coffee there.

She supposed he was regularly seeing Tiffany, but the people he invited for dinner or drinks usually seemed to be business contacts.

Benedict went away for another weekend, and Riley filled in the two days with her brother and his family, helping on the farm and putting out of her mind any thought of where Benedict was and who he was with.

If he was working late in his study, Riley had got into the habit of taking him a cup of coffee before she went to bed. One night she carried a cup through but he wasn't there. Muted music drifted down from the next level, and a light glowed from the open door of the small sitting room there.

Riley went up and paused at the doorway. The center light was off, but a standard lamp cast a soft pale circle, and Benedict lay full length on a wide sofa, his hands clasped behind his head, his eyes closed. The stereo was playing something she vaguely thought was Mozart.

Not sure if he was sleeping, she hovered uncertainly, ready to creep away. And then he opened his eyes as though he'd sensed her presence, and looked at her.

"I disturbed you," she apologized.

His eyes in the dim light at the edge of the lamp's radius were the color of an evening sky, deep and fathomless. "No." He sat up, pushing back his hair with one hand. "Come on in."

He watched her cross the room toward him. Riley was suddenly conscious of the way the stretchy fabric of the knit top she wore with her jeans molded itself to her neatly rounded breasts, and of the fact that she wasn't wearing a bra. It had been hot today and she was more comfortable without.

Not that she'd thought Benedict would notice. When he lifted his eyes and reached to take the cup she held out to him, she decided that he hadn't. His expression was quite detached as he murmured his thanks, and his eyes were almost opaque, despite their dark sheen.

She was about to turn away when he said, "Sit down."

Riley glanced at the empty space beside him, then inquiringly back at him.

His hands cradling the cup, he smiled slightly. "I mean, please sit down, Riley. For a while. I won't bite. That's *your* prerogative."

"I wish you'd stop reminding me of that," she complained, sinking onto the other end of the sofa.

"Am I getting to be a bore on the subject? Sorry, but it was a pretty unique experience for me. Unforgettable."

"Me too. I don't make a habit of going around biting perfect strangers, you know!"

Humor lit his eyes before the lids lowered a little, the subtle gleam intensifying. "What about…men you know well?"

Feeling heat in her cheeks, Riley hoped the light wasn't bright enough for him to see. "I've never bitten a man before!" she said with dignity.

He leaned back, still surveying her from under lazy eyelids. "Then it was the first time for both of us?"

Something intangible hovered between them, like an invisible electrical charge. Or was it her imagination? Benedict had scarcely moved, and his body appeared quite relaxed, legs sprawled before him, his head resting against the high back of the sofa, hands loosely curled about his coffee cup.

The drooping eyelids were probably a result of weariness. "Why don't you have an early night?" she suggested.

Black brows lifted fractionally, his eyes fully open now as he directed a questioning look at her.

"I mean," she said, "I know what long hours you work. Or at least you have been lately."

"I'm not working now," he pointed out. Her heart stopped as he shifted to face her, lifting one arm to lay his elbow and forearm on the sofa back. "What's the matter?" he asked softly. "You're not scared of me, are you?"

"Of course I'm not!" Stupidly, for a moment she'd thought he wanted to touch her. "You're a very thoughtful employer," she told him, reminding herself who he was, what their respective positions were. "Why should I be scared?"

"No reason, of course." Abruptly he lowered his arm, and took a gulp of his coffee. "Only, you seemed nervous."

Riley prevaricated. "When you asked me to sit down I thought maybe you were going to tell me there was something wrong with the way I do my job."

Benedict shook his head. "I just felt like a bit of company. But I mustn't keep you up."

He sounded cool, aloof.

"I don't mind," Riley said quickly. "I mean...I'd

quite like to stay for a while, if that's all right. And
listen to the music with you.''

He looked a little skeptical. "Do you like Mozart?
Or will you be bored rigid?''

"I won't be bored.''

"Want to get yourself a coffee too—or can I pour
a drink for you?'' There was a small corner cabinet
in the room that held a few bottles of liquor.

Riley was unwilling to move. She would make herself a hot chocolate drink before going to bed. "I'm
quite happy.''

He smiled. "So am I.''

They sat in silence until the CD ended. Then Benedict sighed, put aside his empty cup, and got up to
remove the disc.

Riley scooped up the cup and got to her feet. "That
was nice, thank you.''

"Thank *you,* Riley.'' He snapped the disc into its
case and placed it on a rack above the stereo. "For
the coffee and the company.'' Shoving his hands into
his pockets, he stood waiting for her to go.

"Good night,'' she said, making for the door. She
was nearly there before he echoed her, and she
glanced back to throw him a smile.

For some reason he seemed brooding and almost
lonely. She wanted to go back to him and give him
a hug. If he'd been one of her friends she would have
done it, but he was her employer, not her friend, and
he'd think she'd gone nuts.

If he was feeling lonely—and that impression was
probably just a trick of the dim light or her imagination—he was surely capable of doing something
about it.

He'd hired Riley as a housekeeper, not a companion. Tonight he'd just felt like having someone to share the music with. But if he wanted stimulating company—female company—he had only to pick up the phone and call Tiffany. Or if she was unavailable, someone like her.

Riley sighed. She couldn't imagine why the thought was so depressing.

Benedict was busier than ever over the next few weeks. When Riley drove him to work, he was absorbed in his notes and graphs, and if he wasn't dining out he asked her to bring his dinner on a tray to the office.

One night she showered early, put on a nightshirt and covered it with a knee-length, orange satin embroidered kimono that she'd bought in Kyoto, and spent the evening pretending to study while watching a TV movie in her cozy sitting room.

After she'd switched it off she went into the bedroom and was drawing the curtains when she saw a quick small glow stab the darkness outside. Puzzled, she went back through the kitchen to the outside door and peered into the garden.

The light from her window and the kitchen spilled across a tiled area to the lawn, but that only made the darkened periphery seem more black.

She stepped onto the tiles, still slightly warm to her bare feet, crossed to the short grass, and stopped. Then she saw again a tiny orange glow near the pergola.

"Who's there?" she called sharply.

"It's me." The glow arced downward and moved toward her. "Benedict."

"Oh...I'm sorry." Instinctively Riley went for-

ward to meet him. "I didn't know you smoked."
Now she could smell the fragrant, heavy scent.

"The occasional cigar," he answered, looming
nearer in the darkness. "It's a great stress reliever. I
don't do cigarettes anymore."

"You used to?"

"Didn't everyone used to?"

"Not if they had any sense."

"I wasn't long on sense when I was young."

"I don't suppose I was, either," she said candidly.
"I didn't mean to insult you."

"I'm not insulted. Did you come to apprehend an
intruder?"

"Not exactly. I saw the light of the cigar and wondered what it was."

"If anybody's lacking sense—didn't it occur to
you that coming out at night alone to investigate
might be risky?"

He sounded disapproving.

"Well," Riley said, "it didn't actually occur to me
that it was a person until I was already outside. And
when I called out I was all prepared to bolt back into
the house."

"In future I'd appreciate it if you'd call me first
when you see something suspicious, instead of blun-
dering about in the dark on your own."

"You wouldn't have heard me. You were out
here."

"Never lost for an answer, are you? The point is,
what you just did was unsafe. Don't you ever think
before you act?"

"I have a great scream."

The small, breathy sound he made might have been

a laugh. "I remember it well. An amazingly effective weapon. Have you often had cause to practice it?"

"Hardly ever."

"You surprise me," he said dryly.

"Was *that* meant to be an insult?"

"A warning. There may not always be someone to come to your rescue when you put yourself at risk."

"I don't go taking risks for the hell of it."

"No?" He lifted the cigar to his lips and the tip glowed red again.

Riley shifted uneasily, feeling the cool blades of grass between her toes. "I'm sorry if I disturbed your reverie. I suppose you'd rather be alone."

As she made to turn he said, "Why?"

Riley hesitated. "What?"

"Why do you suppose I'd rather be alone?"

"Isn't that why you came out here?"

"I can be alone inside. I started coming out here to smoke because Mrs. Hardy didn't like the smell of cigars in the house. It's become a habit."

"I like the smell," Riley told him. "My father's brother in England used to send him a box of cigars every year at Christmas." He'd smoke one on Christmas Day, one on New Year's Day, and keep the rest for special occasions throughout the year. "Sometimes he'd let me have a puff when my mother wasn't looking."

Benedict laughed. "I can just see you—a tot with a cigar. Come and sit with me, and you can have a puff of mine."

He guided her along the tiled path to where it formed the floor of the little trellised summerhouse. A narrow seat ran around three sides, and the vines made the shadows deeper. Riley perched on the seat and tucked her bare feet up to one side. Benedict sat a couple of feet away and handed her the cigar, already half-smoked. "Here you are."

She sucked in the pungent smoke, savoring the flavor, and blew it out again, then handed it back. "Thanks."

"Finish it if you like."

"No, I was only ever allowed one puff. That's enough to bring back the memories."

"Good memories?"

"Oh, yes."

"You're lucky." He replaced the cigar between his lips.

"I've always thought so. Does that sound smug?"

"No. You said your father *used to* get cigars every year. Is he...not around anymore?"

"Oh, he's fine. Only, his brother died, and my mother wouldn't let him buy them himself. She never did approve of them—didn't want him setting a bad example for us kids."

"The women in your family are a force to be reckoned with, obviously. Is your mother like you?"

"To look at? I guess. We're not a tall family." She recalled that he hadn't liked his own mother very much, and figured it was time to change the subject. "Did Mrs. Hardy bully you?"

"Bully me?" His voice was amused.

"You said she didn't like the smell of cigars—but it's your house, after all."

"She raced around with air fresheners, looking martyred and harassed, and the next day she'd ostentatiously air out the room."

Riley laughed. "That could be intimidating. Does...does Tiffany's father smoke?"

"No."

So perhaps Tiffany too would prefer Benedict to confine his indulgence in the odd cigar to the outdoors.

Benedict stood up, went to the open side of the summerhouse and threw the cigar stub down, crushing it under his shoe. His shadowy form filled the doorway as Riley got up too and went forward, thinking he was ready to leave. But then he turned and faced her, and suddenly the tiny space seemed to shrink still further. There were only inches between them. The aroma of cigar smoke hung in the air, and a lone late cricket chirruped somewhere in the garden.

Riley stepped back again, her legs coming up against the wooden seat.

Benedict raised one hand to the frame of the entrance. "You've never been scared of me," he said roughly.

"I'm not scared."

He muttered something that sounded like, "Maybe you should be."

Chapter Seven

"What?" She must have misheard.

"You said you don't take risks for the hell of it."

Unable to see his expression, Riley fought an unnerving feeling of tension. "I don't."

He gave a short, scornful laugh. "Your trouble is you don't even recognize a risk when it's staring you in the face—and that's surely more dangerous."

"I've no idea what you mean."

"My point exactly. Have you got anything on under that thing?" he enquired harshly.

"What?" Her voice rose to a near squeak.

He shook his head with apparent impatience—even in the dimness she saw the movement. "Your feet are bare," he said accusingly, as if he'd just noticed. "Have you been sitting out here in the cold wearing nothing but that?"

By *that* she supposed he meant the flimsy satin wrap. "I've got a nightshirt on. And I'm not cold."

There was a chill in the night air, and actually her toes were icy, but otherwise she was all right.

"That's open to question," Benedict said darkly, totally confusing her, and finally moved aside. "Get back in the house, for heaven's sake."

He waited for her to pass him, then caught her up and walked at her side. When they'd entered the house he shut the door and locked it before turning to her again. The light made his features look harsh, and she thought it was almost certainly washing all the color from hers. Except that her nose was probably pink from the crisp night air. And of course her hair was hanging about her face in dead-straight strands. She pushed a few back from her eyes, running her tongue over her tooth. "Thanks," she said. "The cigar was nice. Good night."

He was looking at her moodily, but not into her eyes. "Good night, Riley," he said. And he didn't move until she'd gone into her own suite and closed the door.

The following day Riley turned off the air-conditioning as she usually did when Benedict had left the house, worked all morning in shorts and a T-shirt, then had a swim before lunch. Benedict had told her she could use the pool anytime, but she never did when he was around.

She surfaced from a leisurely crawl down the length of the pool, dropped her feet to the bottom as she smoothed her wet hair back with both hands, and found herself staring at a pair of bare, muscular legs.

Her gaze flew past the black swim briefs above the legs to Benedict's face. "What are you doing here?" she gasped.

His brows quirked. "I live here?"

Standing in water that just lapped her breasts, she fought an urge to put her hands over them. Her one-piece swimsuit was perfectly adequate, but it dipped low in the front, and the thin fabric didn't disguise what the cold water had done to her. The effect wasn't helped by the unwelcome, unmistakable stirring of desire that the sight of her near-naked employer had aroused. Did he have to look so damned sexy? "I mean, what are you doing home now?" He never came home for lunch.

"They're redecorating our office building, and I can't concentrate. And a swim seemed a good idea before I get on with some work. Why have you turned off the air-conditioning?"

"Energy saving," Riley said tersely. "I'll turn it on again if you're going to be here." She launched herself into a slow breast stroke toward the steps in a corner of the pool.

"You don't have to get out because I'm here." He had walked along to the steps to meet her. As she climbed them, he offered her his hand, taking her wet one in his strong clasp, then releasing her when she reached the sun-warmed tiles around the pool.

"It's all right." She raised her hands to wring out her hair. Flipping it back, she tried to ignore the fact that he was watching her from under lowered eyelids. It didn't mean a thing. Just idle masculine interest, she guessed, her tongue instinctively going to her crooked tooth. "Do you want lunch?"

"I did say you don't need to make lunch for me." He still wasn't taking his eyes off her, and they looked sort of glazed.

"I haven't had mine yet, so it's no trouble. Is a ham and avocado sandwich okay?"

"If that's what you're having. I'll join you in the kitchen, okay?"

"Whenever you're ready." Riley flashed a smile in his general direction, snatched up a towel and headed for the house, her spine prickling with awareness. She'd reached the doorway and walked into the sudden gloom of the indoors before she heard the splash of Benedict's magnificent body entering the water.

She changed into fresh shorts with a sleeveless top that skimmed her waist, and was placing a plate piled with sandwiches onto the table when Benedict came in, wearing jeans and a white T-shirt that hugged his body, his damp hair slicked straight back.

Riley had plaited hers after toweling it, and secured it with a hair tie. Wet, her hair turned to rats' tails, and anyway she didn't want damp strands falling about her face while she prepared the food.

"Coffee?" she asked as Benedict walked to the table. She'd already made it, and when he nodded, she poured him a cup and another for herself.

He waited for her to sit down. That was one of the things she liked about him. Even though she was his employee, he didn't forget the small courtesies.

And it was nice to be sitting at the table with him again.

"I don't know if you turn off the air-conditioning to save me money or to save the planet," he said, "but it doesn't use a lot of electricity. It's a heat pump—expensive to install but economical to run. I don't want you to be uncomfortable."

"I'm not." She helped herself to a sandwich. "The

house is well insulated, and the pool is great for cool-
ing off.''

"Yes," he said, looking at her rather strangely.
Then he gave a short laugh. "But the effect doesn't
last.''

She was washing up when the young man who
gave the lawns their weekly trim arrived. Through the
kitchen window she saw him trundle the motor
mower to the back lawn.

Benedict might not welcome the noise. She hurried
down the passageway to ask him, tapping on the study
door.

"Come in."

Riley opened the door. "Kevin's here to do the
lawn. Shall I ask him to come back tomorrow? The
motor mower might disturb your work.''

The roar of the mower began outside, and Benedict
said, "I think I can stand it. He won't be long. Thanks
for asking.''

Riley withdrew to her own suite to sit on the window seat that looked out on the back lawn, while she
read the morning's newspaper.

Every now and then she glanced up to idly watch
Kevin push the machine back and forth across the
grass, pausing at one stage to wipe his brow with the
back of one hand and then pull off his T-shirt to re-
veal a tanned chest and muscular arms. It was hot out
there, the sun blazing from a blue, blue sky.

He was quite nice looking—tall and trim and with
fair hair that fell to his broad shoulders. He'd be
maybe twenty or so—a bit young but hardly a boy.
So why didn't Riley feel the faintest echo of the emo-

tions she'd had to battle when Benedict had confronted her at the pool?

Putting down the paper, she stared out the window, seeing powerful shoulders flex as the young man turned the mower, and noting the movement of his haunches under the tight denim of his jeans. She must feel *something* in the face of such male appeal.

Nothing but a sort of distant, aesthetic appreciation.

The mower stopped, and Kevin wiped his brow again, then sauntered over to where he'd left his shirt.

He bent and picked up the discarded shirt, rubbing it over his glistening chest.

That ought to have some effect on her.

The glass between them must make a difference. This was like looking at a moving picture rather than a real man.

Decisively Riley scrambled off the window seat and headed for the kitchen.

A few minutes later she emerged onto the lawn, a foaming mug of cool beer in her hand. Taking a few steps onto the grass, she looked about her, but the mower had disappeared and she couldn't see Kevin.

Then with no warning but a faint hiss, she was drenched in a cold shower of water, momentarily blinded, her skin instantly becoming goosefleshed.

Riley shrieked, and immediately heard an extremely rude word uttered in a startled masculine voice.

Then the water stopped, and Kevin's dismayed face appeared from round the corner where he stood by the master tap on the wall of the house.

"Sorry!" He came pounding toward her as she started to laugh.

Kevin stopped a couple of feet away, relief spreading over his face, and touched her arm. "Are you okay?"

"It's only water." She was still laughing. "I won't melt, but I've already had a swim today, thanks."

"I'm really sorry," he said again. "There's a double attachment on the tap. I thought I was turning on the hose, not the lawn sprinklers—just wanted to cool myself off before I do the front. And I didn't know you were there."

"I was bringing you a cold drink," Riley explained, suppressing her giggles. She held out the mug to him. "I'm afraid your beer's watered."

He took it and grinned back at her. "You're a sport," he said, "taking it this way."

"I must look like a drowned rat." Riley glanced down at her soaked clothing. "I feel like one." Just as well she'd put on a bra after her swim. It was clearly visible through the thin, wet cotton top, but at least the lace cups almost concealed what was underneath them.

"Never seen a rat that looks that good—wet or dry."

Riley's head jerked up. The grin had widened and Kevin was giving her a teasing look. A Hey-you-wanna-play? look.

It seemed she'd finally found a foolproof way to get men to notice she had a woman's body—as long as she didn't mind going round with wet clothes plastered clammily to her skin. First Benedict at the beach, now Kevin. "Thanks," she said, taking a small step backward, "but—"

"Riley!" Benedict's peremptory voice interrupted as he came striding out of the house, looking distinctly annoyed. "Are you all right?"

"Fine," she answered. "The sprinkler system—"

"I saw what happened," he told her curtly, his gaze sweeping over her as he approached them. "You'd better go inside and change. And you—" he glared at Kevin "—can't you be more careful?"

"Yeah, sorry—"

Riley, on her way to the house, turned. "It's no big deal," she said. "Just a mistake—"

"I said, go and change!" Benedict snapped, his brows formidably drawing together.

Tempted to snap right back, Riley remembered who paid her very generous wages and kept a most acceptable roof over her head. She spun round, clamping her mouth tightly shut, and stalked toward the house with her head high.

At the door she paused. Her clothes and hair were still dripping, and she didn't want to leave a trail of water inside the house.

"What are you waiting for?" Benedict demanded, coming back to her side.

Doing her best to sound meek, she said, "Do you think you could bring me a towel please? So I can dry off a bit before going in?"

He cast her an impatient glance and went inside, returning with a large bath towel. "Here."

He stood by while she pulled the tie from her ponytail, rubbed her hair half-dry and dabbed at her arms and legs. Then, holding the towel loosely about her, she stepped into the house.

Benedict was right behind her. "What were you doing out there, anyway?" he asked, following her into the kitchen.

Riley turned to face him. "Taking Kevin a drink. He was hot."

"You'd been watching him."

She wasn't about to admit that, especially when Benedict seemed to think it was a mortal sin. Just as well he didn't know how she watched *him*. "I was reading the paper on the window seat," she said coolly, trying desperately to stop the guilty color rising in her cheeks, "and I noticed he was sweating."

"Do you like sweaty guys?"

Riley blinked. "I just thought he could do with something to cool him down."

Benedict's harsh bark of laughter startled her. "Oh, sure, that would do it all right!"

"What?" Riley was bewildered at his sarcastic tone.

"You swanning out there in your sexy little shorts and minimalist top and offering him a beer," Benedict said. "And then getting yourself soaked to the skin. Seems to be a habit of yours."

What on earth was he accusing her of? "I didn't do it on purpose!"

"*He* might have."

"Oh, that's ridiculous! He didn't even know I was there!"

"Is this the first time you've given him a drink?"

"No." A couple of times she had offered one before Kevin left, and he'd accepted gratefully, downing a fruit juice or a beer before leaving for his next job. "If you're begrudging him a cold drink out of your fridge—"

"I'm not grudging him that!"

"What, then?"

She seemed to have given him pause. "Nothing," he said at last. "But I suggest," he added with unwarranted sarcasm, "that if you're handing out refreshments to every workman who visits the place, you might dress a bit more...well, a bit more!'' His eyes went to the soaked, clinging top.

Her cheeks flaming, she said, ''You told me you didn't care what I wore around the house!''

''I don't. But I didn't expect you to go flaunting yourself in next to nothing—''

Riley gasped with pure rage. Anyone would think she'd been sashaying about in a bikini or something. Her shorts were a snug fit but not excessively brief, and her top was loose and perfectly modest—when it was dry. ''I was taking the man a drink!'' she reiterated between gritted teeth. ''As any decent human being would have. I don't suppose he even noticed what I was wearing—not that it isn't completely respectable.''

Benedict's lip curled. ''Don't kid yourself. Didn't you see the way he was looking at you?''

''What way?'' she asked witheringly. But of course she knew. She'd even been mildly pleased at the implication that she wasn't unattractive. And a bit dismayed that she'd felt no flutter of answering attraction, even without the window between them.

But of course she had just been doused in cold water, the classic cure for erotic longings. Her lips quivered into a smile of amusement. It had been funny, really.

''You know damn well what way!'' Benedict said furiously. ''Are you such a little fool you don't know the risks of inviting that sort of thing?''

He had her pegged as some kind of idiot nymphet. It was so ludicrous, if he hadn't made her hopping mad she'd probably have laughed again. As it was, she felt like spitting at him. Couldn't he see how ridiculous he was being?

She made her eyes round and adopted an expression of coy innocence. "What sort of thing do you mean?" she taunted.

There was an instant when she realized she'd gone too far. His eyes blazed and his hands reached for her. Instinctively she raised her own hands to ward him off, and the towel she was holding dropped to the floor as her head lifted in surprise.

Her palms encountered a warm wall of male chest encased in cotton, and she heard him say in a low, rasping voice, *"Something like this!"*

Then his mouth was covering hers, hot and hungry and electrifying. His arms wrapped about her, lifting her to her toes, and her head was pushed back farther as his lips parted hers.

She felt his breath enter her mouth, and a shaft of pure, hot shivering desire quivered through her body. Her heart hammered in double-quick time, and when she made a small sound of astonished protest in her throat, he lifted one hand and grabbed at her damp hair, holding her head still.

No, she thought. No, this is crazy—he doesn't mean it. And then his other hand slipped to her waist, found the gap between shirt and shorts and slid up her back, then to her breast, cupped in wet lace.

Panic and pleasure warred inside her. What was he doing? What was *she* doing?

Not fighting him, for sure. And she should be. He had no right to do this to her. The kiss was no expression of love—rather of anger. Clenching her fist, she thumped it against his shoulder, summoning righteous rage to her aid. And thumped again, stiffening her body despite its perfidious inclination to nestle into him and welcome the hand that warmed her breast.

She opened her teeth, but before she could close them on his vulnerable lower lip, his mouth abruptly left hers. Still holding her hair, he looked down at her from inches away, his eyes glittering and darkened, but with a spark of savage humor in them. "No, you don't," he said softly. "Not again—not in anger."

Her mouth felt swollen and hot and tingly. She glared at him, straining against his powerful arms. "What the hell do you think you're doing?" she snarled.

He looked startled, and then he smiled at her, the humor in his eyes deepening, and slowly let her go. "I'd have thought that was obvious." He watched her as if expecting to be attacked.

Riley would have liked to attack him, except that she knew he was much stronger than she was—and besides, she was afraid that if he held her in his arms again, she'd simply cave in like a crushed honeycomb.

She took a harsh breath. "If that was supposed to teach me a lesson, you could have saved yourself the trouble. I already know that some men with giant egos see sexual invitations where they don't exist. I'm sure Kevin isn't like that—and I certainly didn't think that *you* were, until now!"

"I'm not." His face had been flushed, like hers, but now it whitened. "Riley, listen to me—"

But she wasn't listening. Without even stopping to pick up the towel, she marched across the kitchen and through the door that led to her private suite, and ostentatiously closed and locked the door behind her, dashing an angry hand over her eyes.

She wasn't crying, dammit. She *never* cried, she despised tears. Being small was bad enough—being small and wimpy and tearful would have been just too awful. She couldn't control her height, but she could control her emotions.

Couldn't she?

She went into the bathroom and stripped off, then turned on the shower. Of course she wasn't dirty, but her skin felt wet and clammy, and the warm water was comforting. The stinging in her eyes must be caused by the force of the water coming from the stainless steel nozzle, and of course the moisture running down her face was from the shower.

Her only consolation was that it wasn't only she who must need a change of clothing. Benedict had clamped her so closely against him that he must have gotten wet, too.

Much later she put his dinner on a tray and carried it to the office. There was no answer to her brisk tap on the door and, after hesitating a moment, she pushed it open.

Benedict was standing at the window, his hands shoved into the pockets of a pair of light twill trousers while he stared outside. He turned when she came in, as if he hadn't heard her knock, and watched her slide the tray onto the desk.

"Thank you," he said formally, and took a step forward. "Riley..."

"Yes?" She folded her hands in front of the thigh-length, straight black skirt and white blouse—legacy of a short-term waitressing job—that she'd dragged from the recesses of her wardrobe, keeping her eyes lowered like a Victorian servant.

"I owe you an apology." His voice was gravelly. "That was despicable behavior, and I assure you it will never happen again."

She guessed that for him it was a pretty hefty wedge of humble pie. What really bothered her was her wholly unwarranted sense of disappointment at his assurance that he would never kiss her again. Struggling with an inappropriate urge to demand to know why not, she judged it safer to say nothing.

"Riley?" he said. "Please look at me."

Riley took a swift little breath and raised her eyes. "I guess it was just a momentary aberration."

Benedict himself had once told her that despite being her employer, he was also a man. Besides, she'd deliberately goaded him. That didn't excuse his behavior, but if she were honest she should accept that her attitude had contributed toward his loss of temper. "I accept your apology." She tried not to sigh.

"Thank you." Benedict looked down at the desk before him and picked up a pen, examining it. "That's all right, then." He put the pen down. "I...er...won't be needing dinner on Wednesday. You can have an extra day off if you like."

Did he want her out of the way? "Thanks," she said. "I might visit my housemates. Ex-housemates." She didn't need to tell him what she was doing in her off time, but she wanted him to know there were no hard feelings so they'd get back to their normal footing. "I could go tomorrow and stay a couple of nights." If he brought Tiffany home she didn't want to be here.

Benedict looked up quickly, then nodded, his eyes going expressionless and opaque. "If you like."

There was a small, uncomfortable silence. Riley broke it. "Eat your dinner before it gets cold," she said, and when she turned to leave he didn't stop her.

Riley's former room in the flat was now occupied by one of Harry's cousins—a young Maori woman studying law at the university, who had been grateful to buy Riley's furniture cheap.

Riley shared dinner with them all, stayed up late talking and watching television, and slept on a camp mattress on the floor of Lin's room. The next evening she volunteered to cook, and afterward they went to a film in town and had coffee in an all-night café.

When she let herself into Benedict's house the following day after her class there was no sign of him. But his bed, as neat as ever, had been slept in.

Riley made it up briskly, and vigorously attacked the rest of the housework. By late afternoon she'd also swum and shopped and been to the library.

Unable to summon any real interest in her latest course assignment, and finding that even her library books failed to hold her attention, she decided to reorganize the kitchen cupboards.

She was headfirst in a lower corner cupboard, her jeans taut over her behind as she tried to fish out a garlic peeler that had rolled into the farthest reaches, when Benedict's voice said, "What on earth are you doing?"

Startled, she jumped, banged her head on the shelf above and gave a yelp of pain before she withdrew from the cupboard and sat back on her knees, a hand to the sore spot.

"Sorry. Are you hurt?" Benedict hesitated, standing just inside the doorway, and she saw the muscles subtly move in his cheeks.

"Just a bruise," she muttered, rubbing at it before dropping her hand. "I was trying to get something out of there. My arms aren't long enough." Following his gaze across the floor, littered with kitchen paraphernalia, she explained, "I can't reach half the stuff in the cupboards, so I'm putting the things I use often into lower ones. I didn't realize it was so late."

A smile glimmered in his eyes as they met hers again, softening his somewhat grim expression. She recalled that the first time she'd asked him to get something from a high shelf he'd looked at her the same way. "You do have problems, don't you?" He ambled over to her, picking his way between the various utensils. "Move over," he ordered.

Riley scooted to the side, and he squatted, stretched an arm into the cupboard and emerged with the peeler in his fingers. "That what you wanted?"

"Thanks." She took it from him. "I'm sorry about the mess, but I've nearly finished. Your dinner will be ready on time."

"Not a problem." Still on his haunches, he looked at her appraisingly. In this position their eyes were almost on a level. Perhaps he found it as novel as she did. "May I eat with you?"

He was asking permission? "Of course," she said. "If you like."

"I like." Benedict still didn't move. Something about her seemed to fascinate him. Then he said, "You have a smudge on your cheek—dust, or a cobweb."

Fascination, huh? Huh. She raised a hand to her face. "Here?"

"A bit higher." He watched her rub at where she thought he was looking. "No." His hand reached out, and she felt his knuckles on the skin over her cheekbone as he gently scrubbed with his thumb. Then his eyes darkened and his thumb stopped moving.

Riley looked back at him, holding her breath, very conscious of his hand against her skin.

"That's it," he said, and his hand fell away. He straightened, and rapidly moved toward the door. But before reaching it he turned. "By the way, I'm expecting a guest from about lunchtime Saturday to Monday morning. We'll be out for dinner on Saturday, but I'd like to invite some other people for Sunday night. Will you mind doing meals for us, and taking days off in lieu next week? It's short notice, so—"

"That's fine." She hoped her voice sounded normal, although her heart was plunging. Dreading the answer, she asked, "Um, which room will the guest be using?"

He shrugged. "Just make up a bed in one of them. It doesn't really matter."

Because the guest would be sharing his bed, anyway?

None of your damned business, she told herself sternly. You knew when you agreed to be Benedict's housekeeper that this was in the cards. You can do it.

Of course she could. Graciously. Efficiently. Like a woman paid to do a job. "A male or female guest?" she enquired innocently.

"Female. Does it make a difference?"

"A woman might appreciate bath oil and extra toi-
letries. Maybe flowers in the room."

"That's thoughtful of you. Flowers would be
nice." And then he was gone, the saloon doors closing behind him.

Picking up a stainless steel stockpot from the litter
on the floor, Riley stared into it as if it were a crystal
ball.

For a minute there she'd thought that something
was happening—or about to happen. Wishful thinking, she decided. Since that kiss she'd been more
aware of Benedict than ever. Now she was reading
things into his behavior that weren't necessarily there.
He'd retrieved an errant utensil for her and removed
a smudge of dirt from her cheek. Those weren't exactly signs of passion.

*Be sensible. As far as he's concerned the kiss was
an appalling mistake, and one he isn't likely to repeat. Last night he was out with Tiffany. She's possibly spending the weekend here. Remember Tiffany
the Gorgeous—the woman he said is all he's ever
wanted? And look at you.*

She shoved the stockpot into the cupboard, flung
several more pots after it and slammed the door on
them, then scrambled to her feet and gathered up the
rest of the things on the floor, piling them into a heap.
They could wait while she prepared dinner for two.

"How's the head?" Benedict asked as she put a
plate of lamb chops and baked potatoes with sour
cream and a dusting of paprika before him.

Riley placed a green salad on the table and sat
down with her own plate. "What?" She'd forgotten
all about that. "Oh, that. Fine." The only thing that

seemed to be aching was a small space about her heart.

"Tough little thing, aren't you?"

"Being brought up with three brothers does that. And I hate being called little."

"I beg your pardon. I should have remembered."

Riley grunted, and helped herself to salad. "How was your evening with Tiffany?" She couldn't help it, she had to know. She gave the bowl a helpful shove toward him.

"Very enjoyable," Benedict said shortly, heaping greens onto his plate. He paused. "What about you?"

Torn between relief that he wasn't waxing fulsome about Tiffany, and unsatisfied curiosity, Riley said with spurious animation, "It was fun. We saw a great film last night."

She launched into an enthusiastic description of the quirky action-comedy-adventure, making him laugh at her description of a couple of scenes. "You'd like it," she assured him.

"Sounds like I would."

And then, remembering, she added hastily, "Tiffany might too."

He looked doubtful. "She likes gentle, romantic films, I think."

"Oh, well…" Riley was quite unable to continue talking about Tiffany. She said brightly, "Harry's modeling agency got him into the Face of the Future contest. The winner gets an audition with an agency in L.A., and it'll be on TV so it's great exposure, even if he isn't placed."

"Harry's a model?"

"Part-time, but this could boost his career. Isn't it terrific?"

"Terrific." Benedict turned his attention back to his chops, sawing at one with unnecessary force considering that it was really quite tender.

On Saturday Riley did her marketing early, arriving back with bags of fresh produce. Benedict's car wasn't in the garage, but later she heard it, and then his voice in the distance before a door shut on the sound.

Riley had prepared the room opposite the master bedroom before she left, placing a bowl of flowers on the dressing table. She wondered if it had been a waste of time.

Benedict had asked her to serve lunch for him and his guest on the terrace. It was cooler there at midday. "Keep it simple and light," he suggested. "Save your energy for dinner tomorrow."

Riley made a dish of mixed raw vegetables and thinly sliced cold meats to serve with crusty French bread and a jug of light dressing, with freshly baked muffins to follow. She set a cloth on the outdoor table, laying two places, and when she took out the food Benedict was already pouring wine for his visitor.

"Riley." He put down the glass and stood up. "This is my good friend, Mrs. Sato. She flew in from Japan this morning. Mrs. Sato taught me to speak Japanese."

Mrs. Sato smiled graciously. "How do you do." Her dark eyes were almost hidden behind large tinted glasses. Although her skin was smooth and there was no gray in her carefully arranged hair, Riley guessed she was middle-aged.

"Really?" Riley gave the woman a dazzling smile before placing the platter on the table. Glad she had decided to don the waitress uniform today, she stepped back, flattened her hands against her thighs and bowed with the correct depth and deference to Mrs. Sato, greeted her in Japanese and added fluently in the same language, "If I had known our guest was from Japan I would have prepared something different."

The older woman smiled with delight. "This looks delicious. I can eat Japanese food at home."

Benedict was staring at Riley. "You didn't tell me you speak Japanese!"

"You didn't tell me *you* did, either," Riley retorted.

Mrs. Sato laughed. "Benedict speaks it well," she said in her precise English. "He was a very good pupil, very intelligent."

I'll bet he was, Riley thought as she returned to the kitchen. Japanese, huh? The Japanese market was frequently touted as New Zealand's future, but most businessmen relied on interpreters. Learning the language was another indication of Benedict's determination to succeed in any goal he set himself.

After lunch he brought in the dishes himself. "Where did you learn Japanese?" he asked her curiously.

"In Tokyo, teaching English."

"I thought you weren't qualified yet."

"They just wanted basic and conversational English and were recruiting young English speakers from all over the world. I read about it in England and applied. It paid my fare to New Zealand. I'd always had this dream of returning here someday. There's a big demand for ESL teaching in New Zealand, and I'd enjoyed it so much in Japan, I decided to go for it as a career.''

''And when you're qualified, you'll leave me.''

Riley's eyelids flickered at his almost accusing tone. ''It won't be until next year, at least.'' And if he was going to marry Tiffany—or anyone else—she didn't intend to stick around.

On Sunday evening Tiffany and her parents were among the dinner guests. Tiffany greeted Riley with her usual friendliness, and added, ''If you need any help out there, let me know.'' She turned to Mrs. Sato. ''Riley took over from Benedict's previous housekeeper at a moment's notice,'' she informed the visitor, ''and she made us a wonderful meal.''

''Thank you,'' Riley murmured.

She was about to take the dessert to the dining room when there was a knocking on the back door. She wondered who was calling at this hour.

Harry stood there with Rosalita in his arms. ''Can we come in?''

''I'm awfully busy. Benedict's having a dinner party—''

''We won't get in the way, will we, Rosalita?''

Riley stepped back and closed the door behind them. ''Hi, sweetie.'' She kissed Rosalita's cheek and was rewarded by an ecstatic smile.

''I'll keep her quiet,'' Harry promised. He put a finger to his lips and looked at Rosalita. ''Shh, baby.''

Rosalita tried to imitate him, pursing her lips and blowing on her finger.

Riley laughed.

''We'll go into your rooms,'' Harry offered, ''and wait until you're done.''

"No, you can talk to me while I'm working. I have to take dessert in but I'll be back soon."

As Riley picked up the heavy cut-glass bowl, Tiffany came through the swing doors.

"I know you said you didn't need help, Riley," she said gaily, "but I thought— Oh!" She broke off, seeing Harry standing there, and seemed transfixed, her blue eyes widening and her luscious lips parting in silent wonder.

Chapter Eight

Harry did have that effect on women at first sight. Riley had got over it after a few weeks of sharing a flat with him and discovering that he sometimes forgot to remove his underwear from the bathroom floor, never remembered to lower the toilet seat and snored loudly enough to provoke his housemates into banging on the wall of his room to shut him up.

"Oh, hello, *gorgeous!*" Tiffany warbled, and floated across the room, arms outstretched. After a second Riley realized that it was Rosalita she was heading for. "Will she come to me?"

Rosalita clutched at Harry's shirt and buried her face in it.

"She's shy!" Tiffany backed off a little and fluttered her lashes at Harry. "Is she yours?"

"Yes!" There was something oddly vehement about Harry's tone.

Riley introduced them.

Tiffany seemed to have forgotten all about helping

Riley serve the meal. Rosalita had briefly lifted her face to give this new person a tentative grin and was now playing peekaboo while Tiffany cooed over her.

"I have to take this to the dining room," Riley said loudly, and headed for the door with the dessert bowl.

"Oh—you don't really need me, do you?" Tiffany asked.

"Not at all." Riley began to back through the swing door. "But *Benedict* might wonder where you are."

Heavens, she sounded like a disapproving school-mistress, she thought, catching Tiffany's astonishment before the doors swung shut again and Riley turned to march down the passageway.

Entering the dining room, she placed the dessert on the table. Benedict glanced behind her but didn't ask where Tiffany was. He probably thought she was using the bathroom.

When Riley returned to the kitchen, Rosalita was nestled in Tiffany's arms, trying to snatch at tantalizing golden curls.

Reluctantly releasing the baby to her father, Tiffany said, "I suppose I'd better be getting back to the table."

"I'm sure they're missing you," Riley told her.

She wasn't sure what the quizzical look the other woman threw her was supposed to mean, but she had other things to think about. Waiting until Tiffany was well out of earshot, she demanded, "What are you doing here, Harry?"

Harry gave her his dazzling male-model smile. "Rosalita missed you last time you visited."

"Of course I'm delighted to see Rosalita," Riley said.

Hearing her name, Rosalita turned and held out her arms to Riley. Accepting the invitation, Riley added to Harry, "And you too. But isn't it late for her to be up?"

Harry was staring at Rosalita as if he was afraid to take his eyes off her. Lifting them to Riley, he said, "Do us a favor, Ri? Let us stay the night."

"Sure," she said hesitantly. "What's up?"

"Tell you later," he promised, relief spreading over his face. "Can you hold her while I get some stuff out of the van?"

Just as Riley began to wonder if she'd been left literally holding the baby, he returned with a pile of blankets and toys in his arms.

They reversed the high-backed two-seater against the wall to make a safe bed for Rosalita, and Riley told Harry, "There's a spare bed in my room." She hoped his snoring wouldn't keep her awake.

"I've got a sleeping bag," he said. "I'll bunk down in here with Rosalita."

"I have to serve the coffee. If you want anything, help yourself. Benedict won't mind as long as you don't eat him out of house and home." And anyway, she always meticulously made up from her own pocket any inroads her friends had made.

"Riley," Harry said urgently as she was about to leave, "don't tell anyone we're here, okay?"

Riley's tongue teased her odd tooth. "All right," she said reluctantly, not reminding him that Tiffany knew, anyway.

After serving the coffee, she peeked into her sitting room and saw that it was darkened, but Harry was singing softly, his shadowy form bent over the reversed sofa, while Rosalita gave a sleepy whimper.

Quietly Riley closed the door again, and didn't return until she'd finished for the night and cleared the kitchen.

Leaving the light on, she opened the suite door.

Harry was a long, huddled shape in a sleeping bag on the floor, but as she opened the door he quickly sat up. "Riley?" he muttered.

She kept her voice low, not wanting to wake Rosalita. "Who else?"

He lay down again, but she whispered, "Harry—you've got to talk to me! Come out here."

"What if your boss comes in?"

So what? Why was he so anxious not to be seen? Still, she didn't want Benedict to interrupt while Harry was finally satisfying her increasingly uneasy curiosity. "My bedroom, then," she suggested.

Harry eased himself out of the sleeping bag and followed her through to her room.

Riley turned on the light and sat on her bed, leaning against the headboard with folded arms while Harry sank down on the other end. He'd stripped to a pair of amazing tiger-striped satin undershorts, but she was too worried to appreciate how terrific he looked. "Harry, have you kidnapped Rosalita?"

A hunted look appeared in his eyes, but his voice was defiant. "How can I kidnap my own child?" Then he said grudgingly, "Aneta wants to take her away."

Riley gasped. *"Why?"*

"She met this guy. Some Californian. He wants to marry her and adopt Rosalita and take her to live with them in America." His wonderful dark eyes turned stormy. "Rosalita's *mine*."

"And Aneta's," Riley reminded him carefully. "She'll be worried out of her mind!"

"She knows Rosalita's safe with me. I left a note at the flat for her," Harry said. "She was picking her up tonight. I've got to keep my baby, Riley! I was going to take her to my auntie's but Aneta knows all the rellies—she'd look there. You won't give us away, will you?" His eyes pleaded.

"Oh, Harry!" Riley scooted over to sit near him, touching his arm. "You know you can't do this."

His dark eyes turned to her, and she saw tears in them. "I love her so much."

"I know." She slid her arms about his bare waist, giving him a comforting cuddle, and felt his strong, weight-toned arms go about her in return. He clung to her, his breath coming in sobbing gasps. "I know," she repeated, patting him soothingly. "But you have to take her back to her mother, Harry, before the two of you can try to sort something out."

After a long while he gave a shuddering sigh and became heavy in her arms. "Yeah," he groaned. "I s'pose."

Riley kissed his cheek, and eventually he eased away from her, rubbing a hand over his eyes. "I just sort of panicked, you know? Can we still stay for tonight?" he begged. "I don't want to disturb Rosalita again and—" his voice shook "—I don't know how many more times I'll get to have her with me."

"On one condition." Riley gestured to the bedside telephone. "Call Aneta." As he hesitated, she said, "You know she'll be out of her mind. Besides, there's a chance she hasn't contacted the police yet. You don't want it on record that you took Rosalita. You could lose all contact if you're convicted of kidnapping."

"Would you talk to her?" he asked. "I don't want to right now, and if *you* tell her Rosalita's okay—"

"What's the number?" Riley asked with relief.

She woke to the sound of Rosalita crowing wordlessly, followed by Harry's deep murmur. Riley made toast fingers spread with Marmite, and Harry fed the baby in the big kitchen while she sat on his knee.

"Can you keep an eye on her until Aneta comes?" Harry asked as he put Rosalita down and she toddled back through the half-open door to her toys in Riley's sitting room. The Californian boyfriend had volunteered to drive Aneta over this morning. "I can't stand handing her over to that—that American."

"You're handing her to her mother, Harry—just like you always do." But she could see how he was feeling. "All right," she relented.

"They won't be long." Harry refused the coffee Riley had poured for him and gave her a hug. "You were brilliant last night, Riley. I don't know what I'd have done without you," he told her gruffly.

Riley returned the hug. "Go on, you know any woman would do anything for you," she teased gently.

"I wish." Slowly he loosened his hold. "Tell that to Aneta, would you? Please?"

"I can try." She laid her hand on his chest to give it a friendly pat. "But you're going to have to talk to her yourself, eventually."

"Yeah." He sighed, letting his arms drop. "I guess."

Riley kept one of hers about him as she walked him to the door.

Closing it behind him, she turned to lean on it, then immediately straightened as Benedict shouldered through the saloon doors at the other side of the room.

He was wearing light track pants and a T-shirt, and there was a faint sheen of sweat on his forehead.

"Good morning," Riley said.

Benedict returned her greeting rather curtly and crossed to the coffee machine. "Is this yours?" he asked, seeing the filled cup already there beside it.

"No," Riley answered. "You can have it. How was your run?" she asked him politely.

"Fine. Thanks," he added grudgingly, and took a swig of the coffee.

From her suite, a fretful wail came.

Benedict stiffened. Riley headed for the doorway.

Rosalita was clinging to the sofa, trying to reach a ball that had rolled into the corner. "Sorry, hon." Riley handed her the ball and picked her up. "I didn't mean to neglect you."

When she turned, Benedict was standing in the doorway, looking thunderous.

"You don't mind me baby-sitting for a while, do you?" she asked him nervously. "Her mother's coming soon to pick her up."

He scowled at the child. "I suppose not."

"Da?" Rosalita said. "Dadda?"

"Daddy's gone to work," Riley told her. "But your mother's coming to fetch you. That's probably her now," she added as someone knocked on the back door.

When she brought Aneta and her male companion through to pick up Rosalita's paraphernalia, Benedict was leaning against the sink counter, finishing his coffee.

He nodded at Riley's brief introduction, and watched her see the others out. She went to the car with them and kissed Rosalita goodbye, but there was no chance to talk to Aneta alone. The boyfriend seemed in a hurry to leave.

When she returned, Benedict was still where she'd left him, cradling the coffee cup in his hands. "Where's her father?" he said.

"He didn't want to meet her mother's boyfriend." Frowning anxiously, she said, "Aneta's thinking of marrying him and moving to America with Rosalita."

He gave her a sharp glance. "You don't seem to like the idea?"

"Harry's devastated!"

"I'm sure you were a great comfort to him."

There was something in his tone that she couldn't put her finger on. "I certainly hope so," she returned rather defiantly.

"I came to thank you last night for serving my guests a magnificent dinner, but your door was closed and I didn't want to disturb you."

"Thanks," she said mechanically. "Did Tiffany mention that Harry and Rosalita were here?"

"Yes, she mentioned it," he said austerely, and turned to rinse his cup, not bothering with the dishwasher, and laid it on the drainer. "By the way," he said, going toward the swing doors, "you'd be wise to draw your curtains at night. The neighborhood isn't immune to Peeping Toms."

Draw her curtains? Riley was sure she'd done that before going to bed. She always did when she was undressing. "I do," she said as the doors swung to behind him with a whoosh. Over the top of them she watched his dark head recede down the passageway.

He probably hadn't heard.

That afternoon she visited Aneta and Rosalita.

"I promised Harry," she told Benedict guiltily, arriving home late after an exhausting afternoon, "that I'd go and—"

"Never mind," he interrupted her breathless explanation. He wasn't in the best of moods, she could see. He'd thrown open the internal door as she was parking in the garage, and waited for her to enter the house, almost like an irate father. "You could have phoned. You're not a slave, Riley, and you're owed some time off. I was just...concerned that something might have happened to you."

"I'm sorry," she said for the third time since she'd arrived. "I'll get dinner on right away. It should be ready in half an hour."

That week she hardly saw him, and if he was home he treated her with aloof courtesy when he wasn't hunched over the computer in his study.

Taking both Tuesday and Wednesday off, she visited an elderly ex-landlady she'd boarded with for a while when she first arrived in Auckland, did some shopping and lunched with friends.

On Thursday Benedict told her he wouldn't be coming home the following day. "I'm spending the weekend on Tiffany's father's yacht," he said.

"That's nice," she said brightly. "It'll be good for you, having some real time off. I hope you're not taking your computer with you." He was practically wedded to the thing lately. "Going anywhere in particular?"

"The plan is to sail up to the Bay of Islands. We cast off Friday afternoon, so you can have three days off. You're due some extra time."

The Bay of Islands—beautiful, historic, idyllic. And romantic. Were he and Tiffany going alone, or with her parents? She couldn't ask him point-blank. "Sounds lovely. Um…my brother will be in town with his family this weekend. They're taking the kids to Rainbow's End. I was hoping to spend some time with them." She hesitated, then decided to take the plunge. "I wouldn't have asked if you were going to be here, because of the children, but would you mind if they stayed with me? It would save them paying for a motel, and the kids are very good. I'll keep them away from the main house—"

"No problem." He almost seemed pleased at the idea. "Just watch them around the pool. They're welcome to use it, but not unsupervised."

"Thank you, Benedict. You're very generous."

He shrugged. "I'm not going to be using it."

"And you're no dog in the manger, are you?" she said lightly.

For some reason he scowled. "No." He was looking at her, but she guessed he must have been thinking about something else. "No," he repeated as if he needed to convince himself. "I'm not."

Riley was glad she had company for the weekend. Keeping track of two lively children and catching up with her brother and sister-in-law helped her to stop thinking about Benedict and Tiffany sailing together on her father's yacht. To the romantic Bay of Islands. For two whole days—and nights.

On Saturday evening she volunteered to mind the children, shooing their parents out for a night on the town. When they came home, looking soft-eyed like a pair of honeymooners, she made her way upstairs. Benedict had suggested she use one of the guest bedrooms for the weekend and leave the suite for her brother and his family.

Late on Sunday afternoon she waved them goodbye and returned to the house, sitting down quietly with a cool drink and the Sunday paper that her brother had left. When she'd finished reading she went upstairs to tidy the guest room and bathroom she'd used, and decided to change Benedict's bed while she was about it and wash the lot together.

She was making it up with clean sheets when she heard a door close downstairs. Benedict must be home.

As she was smoothing the cover back on his bed he appeared in the doorway. A nylon overnight pack swung from his hand, and he looked fit and slightly tousled in an open-necked knit shirt, cotton pants and deck shoes. He might have stepped out of an ad for expensive casual wear.

He dropped the bag on the floor and leaned on the doorjamb, smiling at her. "Hi." His eyes were bright and he looked happy.

"Hi." Riley stooped to pick up the discarded sheets. "You're earlier than I expected. I'll be out of here in a minute."

"No hurry. How was your weekend?"

"Great. I have messages for you from my brother and his family. Thank you so much for letting them use your home, and they left you a little present to show their appreciation.''

''No need for that.''

He had everything he wanted, but she'd suggested a packet of cigars; she'd taken note of the particular brand that Benedict occasionally smoked. ''How was the cruising?'' she forced herself to ask.

''Fantastic sailing,'' he said offhandedly. ''Couldn't have asked for better weather. A good stiff breeze all the way.''

She didn't want to know about the sailing and the weather. But then she didn't want to know about him and Tiffany, either. ''I'm so glad you enjoyed it,'' she said with all the false warmth she could inject into her voice. ''You should do that sort of thing more often.''

''You think so?'' He looked at her searchingly. Then for some reason he sighed, taking his hand from the doorjamb and picking up his bag to cross the room. ''Tiffany said that too.''

''Tiffany's right,'' Riley said without a tremor. ''All work and no play, you know…''

''Am I dull, Riley?'' He regarded her questioningly. ''Boring?''

''No, of course you're not!'' She hugged the bundle of sheets to her chest. ''Tiffany doesn't think so, does she?''

His eyes flickered. ''If she does she's careful not to show it.'' He gave a rather weary smile. ''She even makes an effort to seem interested when I talk about my basketball team or business. What about you?''

''Me?'' Astonished, she asked, ''What does it matter what I think? But you're not,'' she added hastily. ''Boring, I mean. Not a bit!'' Riley enjoyed their conversations, even when he talked about his work and she couldn't always follow the technicalities. She liked his enthusiasm and intensity, and had to admire the way he'd set himself goals and then fulfilled them. All in all he was an interesting, complex person. And that didn't even take into account the raw sex appeal that no amount of sophistication and expensive dressing could stifle. Of course he wasn't a bore.

"But then you'd have to say that, wouldn't you?" Benedict mused, his eyes rather piercing. "Me being your employer and paying your wages. I shouldn't have put you on the spot."

"That has nothing to do with it," Riley protested. "Honestly!"

"Then why don't you—" He broke off. "Why don't you get on with what you're doing, and I'll see you later," he said.

She hesitated, looking at the bag he still held. "Do you have things in there for washing?"

He looked down as though he'd forgotten about it. "I already left them on the washing machine."

"What would you like for dinner?" she asked, on her way to the door.

"It's still your day off. What do you say to fish and chips from the takeaway? Or do you have your own plans for dinner?"

"I'm not going anywhere." She'd enjoyed her visitors, but now they were gone she was quite tired. "Fish and chips sounds good."

"I'll get them," Benedict promised, "as soon as I've cleaned up. You're not in a hurry, are you? I thought I might walk. Find my land legs again."

"Can I come?" she asked impulsively. A walk

with Benedict in the cool of the early evening seemed like just what she needed, despite her tiredness.

"Sure," he said. "If you like."

They walked briskly to the fish and chip shop, and left it just at dusk, with a well-wrapped parcel tucked into the curve of Benedict's arm. Taking a shortcut through a small, deserted park, Benedict said, "I'm hungrier than I thought. The smell is driving me crazy."

Riley laughed. "We could eat it here," she suggested, indicating a bench placed invitingly under one of the big totara trees around the park's perimeter. "If you can't wait."

He looked at her. "Good idea." Leaving the path, he headed across the grass toward the bench. "Besides, by the time we get home it'll need reheating."

Riley followed, and helped him empty the brown paper bag and open the white-wrapped packages inside.

They ate with their fingers, licking them afterward, and Benedict screwed up the greasy paper and tossed it accurately into a nearby rubbish basket.

Riley applauded. "Good shot!"

He turned, grinning at her. The tree overhead shadowed his face, but she could see his white teeth, the flash of his eyes. Her heart seemed to turn over, and a strange feeling came over her, a muddled combination of sheer pleasure in just sitting here close by him, and a tearing sadness at the transience of the moment.

There was a second when everything stilled, even time. Riley stopped breathing and Benedict's grin disappeared. Something shimmered in the air between them, enveloped them in an invisible capsule of awareness. Her lips parted involuntarily, and he began to bend his head toward her. She knew he was going to kiss her, the glow in his eyes told her so, and she turned up her mouth expectantly, longing for the touch of his.

Then a dog barked, and an elderly couple with a Labrador on a lead entered the park, walking briskly arm in arm.

Benedict jerked away from her, shattering the spell.

Disappointment almost choking her, Riley remembered Tiffany, and Benedict's avowed determination not to be diverted from his life goals. Jumping up, she began walking away, hardly knowing what she was doing, except she had to get away quickly before she flung herself into his arms and begged him to kiss her.

"Riley?"

She darted to the swings, took one and pushed off, swiftly arcing out of his reach as he drew near.

Since childhood she'd loved to swing. There was something about the air rushing against her face, the ground falling away below, the glimpses of a panoramic view of the world as she pumped with her legs, felt the balance of her body alter and control the swing. And she needed this now, a purely physical activity to dispel the depression that threatened to settle on her like an invisible, suffocating cloak.

She closed her eyes, letting her head tip back as she drove her feet forward, pointing to the darkening sky, just to feel the rhythm of her passage as she soared higher, until a delicious, tiny thrill of fear trembled through her body. And she opened her eyes to see Benedict watching her, his hands in his pockets, his face closed and brooding.

When Riley felt she had regained some emotional equilibrium, she let the momentum slow, and gradually the arcs grew shorter and shorter until she was able to put her feet to the ground and stop.

"Sorry to keep you waiting." She pushed her hair from her eyes as she rejoined Benedict. Her cheeks felt glowing and her eyes alert, stinging. She was on an artificial adrenaline high. "I guess it's childish, but I can never resist a swing," she said. "It sort of gives you a new view of the world, from up there."

"I know the feeling."

"About swings?" she queried.

"Not swings." When she turned back to him he was looking at her, not smiling but with a strange quirk at the corner of his mouth. "New views of the world."

Riley's brow creased. "I'm not sure what you're talking about."

"I'm not sure that I know, myself," he confessed. "Except that I almost made a huge mistake."

"Oh." She plunged back into depression. Well, she'd known it was a mistake, hadn't she? In the gathering darkness maybe she'd looked pretty good to him, momentarily. But then, like her, he'd remembered Tiffany and now he was probably blessing the interruption.

Chapter Nine

For the rest of the walk home Benedict seemed to withdraw into silence. Riley lengthened her stride and kept her mouth firmly shut.

Consequently she was panting by the time Benedict opened the front door for her and stood back to let her in.

"Was I going too fast for you?" he asked. "Why didn't you say so?"

"It's good exercise," Riley replied lightly. "Don't worry about it." She stifled a yawn with her hand.

"You're tired."

"I had a hectic weekend," she admitted. "I guess you'll be tired too. Do you want coffee?"

"I'll take some into the study." He accompanied her to the kitchen and said, "Instant will do. I'll get my own. Do you want a cup?"

"No, thanks." She had a drink of water while he put on the kettle.

"Have an early night," he advised her.

She supposed it was a dismissal. "Thanks for the fish and chips," she offered. "Good night, Benedict."

"Good night."

She felt him watching her walk away from him. As she entered her suite and closed the door, her phone began ringing, and she hurried to pick it up. "Hello?"

"Riley?" Harry didn't wait for her to confirm it. "Aneta said you made her see that it mightn't be good for Rosalita, to take her away from me."

"I didn't say that, exactly—"

"You told her I was a good father and Rosalita loves me."

"I'm sure she already knew that." Riley couldn't remember half of what she'd said. Mostly she'd just listened. And had come away feeling that Aneta wasn't in love with her Californian. Flattered by his proposal and tempted at the thought of a new life and apparent security for herself and her child, but torn about leaving her family.

"I asked her to marry me," Harry said, "again."

"What did she say?"

"She wants time to decide. When Rosalita was on the way, our families were both pressuring us to get married, and she figured that was why I'd asked her then."

"Are you in love with Aneta?"

Harry was silent for a few seconds. "I love her," he said finally. "We were in love when we made Rosalita, but then we both got scared and angry. We sort of lost each other. Now she thinks I'm just saying it to keep Rosalita."

"Well, I suppose you'll have to show her that you mean it," was all Riley could suggest.

"Yeah. She did say she'll come to the show on Wednesday. Will you be there?"

The Face of the Future contest. She'd bought a ticket but had forgotten to check with Benedict. "Of course. Wouldn't miss it for anything."

"I'd really like to go," she told Benedict next morning, hating the thought of letting Harry down. "You don't have anything on that night, do you?"

He was staring at her in a rather strange way. "I've arranged to have dinner out with Tiffany. There's…something I have to talk to her about."

Riley swallowed a familiar ache in her throat. "You won't be needing me, then," she said sturdily.

"No," Benedict said. "I suppose not." He cleared his throat. "Wish Harry the best of luck for me."

Riley met Aneta and her former housemates outside the contest venue, and they trooped to their second-row seats together. Each time Harry appeared to strut his stuff before the judges they whistled and clapped, and in the final minutes of the male section they collectively held their breaths while the third and second places were announced.

Then the guest compere read out Harry's name, and they all leaped to their feet cheering, squealing, and sharing hugs with one another and with Harry's family, who were on their feet too.

They all went back to the house to celebrate with friends, relatives and well-wishers until the early hours, and Riley eventually crashed on a mattress on the floor of Lin's room, dragging herself out in the morning and driving to Benedict's place just in time to see him back his car out of the garage.

She drew up on the road, and gave him a cheerful wave that he didn't return. As she turned into the drive he took off with an uncharacteristic roar and a screech of tires.

Maybe his dinner with Tiffany hadn't gone well, she thought hopefully, and then castigated herself for being mean-minded.

The day passed slowly. It was raining when she left her polytech class, and still raining when she returned from visiting a friend at the other side of the city, although now it had turned into a misty drizzle.

She heard Benedict's car arrive and was wondering if he'd be in for dinner when there was a knock on the outer kitchen door and Harry burst in, holding an enormous bouquet of mixed flowers wrapped in cellophane. His hair and the flowers were beaded with tiny raindrops, and when he saw Riley he smiled, came straight to her and kissed her cheek with cold, damp lips. "These are for you," he said.

Taking the extravagant bundle, Riley laughed in astonishment. "What on earth for?"

"For talking to Aneta, of course. *He's* going back to America. She turned him down."

"Poor guy," Riley murmured.

"Yeah." Harry grinned. "Breaks my heart."

She gave him a reproving look. "I hope you bought flowers for Aneta too."

Harry's grin widened. "Red roses. They're in the van."

Riley bent her head to sniff at the bouquet. "These are lovely. Thank you."

"I got a little posy for Rosalita too—real cute. Wanna see it?"

"Love to." The rain had almost stopped, and she walked with him to the road.

Harry opened the passenger door and she glimpsed a huge bouquet of roses as he turned, holding a tiny red, white and yellow bouquet of carnations nestled into a gold doily and tied with a huge red bow. A miniature stuffed clown formed the centerpiece of the arrangement, its striped suit and bright-yellow hair matching the flowers.

"Rosalita will love it!" Riley assured him. She'd probably tear the bouquet to bits if she was allowed to, but it was a neat idea, and maybe she'd settle for the clown to play with.

Harry put the posy carefully back on the seat and closed the door. "I'm really grateful to you, Riley." He kissed her cheek again. "I'm going to get that woman to marry me," he vowed. "Someday."

Riley gave him a nice warm hug and returned the kiss. "Good luck."

She waited on the path until he'd started the engine, waving to him before turning to walk back to the house. Smiling, she briefly clasped her hands over her head in a gesture of victory, and executed a little skipping step before taking the path to the back of the house. It was nice to see Harry happy again.

In the kitchen she picked up the bouquet and looked for a container, but couldn't find anything large enough.

There was a big pottery urn in the main lounge. If she put the flowers into that Benedict could enjoy them too.

With the bouquet in her arms, she had entered the double doors of the lounge and was already crossing to the corner where the container stood when she realized that Benedict was standing at a window with his back to her.

"Oh!" She stopped short as he turned. "Sorry—I didn't mean to disturb you."

He was holding a shot glass with a half inch of amber liquid in it. "Harry?" he enquired, glancing at the flowers.

"How did you know?"

"Saw him leave just now." He tipped the glass to his mouth and swallowed. "How did he get on last night?"

Riley's face lit up. "He won! Isn't it great?"

Benedict didn't look as if he thought so. But he said, "That means he goes to America?"

"Only for an audition, but if they like him, who knows where that might lead. Though it could make things a bit complicated," she added thoughtfully, thinking of Aneta and Rosalita. "He wants to get married."

Benedict had started to raise the glass again. It stopped in midair so suddenly that the remaining liquid sloshed up the sides. Then he completed the movement and downed the lot. "Married?" he said hoarsely.

He shouldn't have drunk the liquor so fast. "Yes," Riley said. "And if he got a job over there…" Maybe Aneta and Rosalita would be moving to America after all, if Harry could persuade her.

"I suppose you'd be pleased, wouldn't you?"

"Well, whatever he wants."

"Lucky guy." He sounded grumpy. Harry's problems obviously didn't interest him. He looked at the flowers again, his expression hardly appreciative.

"I was going to put these in that pottery thing."
Riley indicated a big container in one corner.

"They're your flowers."

"I don't mind sharing." Riley smiled at him.

"I do."

Riley's eyes widened. "Pardon?"

"They're yours," he said, almost with loathing.
"Put them in your own rooms for God's sake."

"Oh." Riley flushed. Did he feel she was en-
croaching? "I thought you might like—"

"I just told you, I *don't* like. Take the damned
things away! And I won't be wanting dinner tonight."
He strode over to the drinks cabinet, picked up an
opened bottle and poured more into his glass, immediately throwing half of it down his throat.

He was drinking whisky. That was unusual.

Already on her way to the door, Riley stopped.
"Don't you think you should have something to eat?
If you're going to keep drinking at that rate—"

"What the hell do you care?" He swung round to
face her. "You're my housekeeper, remember? Not
my bloody guardian angel."

Riley took a step backward. She ought to leave him
and his mood, but it was unlike Benedict to be so
boorish. He was usually so careful to be courteous—
cultivated as part of his painfully built image, she'd
guessed, when he'd repudiated his rough background
and hauled himself into the world of respectability.

Something must have gone badly wrong. "Have
you had a fight with Tiffany?" she asked him.

Benedict gave a crack of harsh laughter. "Tiffany
doesn't fight. She's probably never raised her voice
in her life. And," he added savagely, "she'd never
bite a man."

Couldn't he forget about that? Riley shifted her feet uncertainly, not sure what to say next. "What is it, then?" She hated to leave him alone this way. "Benedict, what's wrong?"

"Nothing." He spun away from her and went to the window again, downing more of his whisky. "Everything," he muttered under his breath, but Riley heard.

Carefully she placed the flowers on a table and went toward him. "If I can help…"

"You?" He tossed her a decidedly unfriendly glance. Then he looked away again.

She touched her tooth, moistened her lips. "Whatever it is, if you want to talk—"

He gave a bark of derisive laughter. "If I did you're the last person I'd want to talk to."

Riley tried not to be hurt. He was upset and probably didn't realize what he was saying. "Tiffany, then?" she suggested with an effort. If he hadn't fought with her, perhaps something else was wrong, and he needed her. "I could phone her, if you like."

"No!" He turned again and glared at her. "I *don't…want…Tiffany!*"

Riley smiled a little sadly. "But you do—you said so."

"I know what I said. She's the perfect woman— sweet, biddable, at home in the best circles. And I'm the biggest damn fool in creation." He finished his drink and banged the glass down on the broad windowsill. Lifting his head again, he looked at Riley with bleak eyes. "I won't be marrying Tiffany. I won't be marrying anyone."

Light dawned. He'd proposed last night—the something important he'd had to say to her—and Tif-

fany had turned him down. He thought he'd made a
fool of himself by aspiring to marry her.

No wonder he was in such a foul mood. And here
Riley had been wittering on about flowers and Harry
and his projected marriage. "Oh, Benedict!"

She suffered a most extraordinary range of emotions within less than a second—huge relief, unwarranted hope, compunction and guilt, and then wrench-
ing sympathy. Benedict was obviously shattered.

There was only one thing she could do, and Riley
did it without thinking—swiftly she closed the space
between them and slipped her arms about him. "I'm
so sorry!"

"Riley—" His voice was muffled. "What are you
doing?"

"Comforting you," she said quietly.

"Riley—" he said unsteadily "—Riley, don't!"

Was he crying? She looked up. His eyes were dry
but tortured, his cheeks pale. "It's all right," she said.
"You ought to let your emotions go sometimes. You
dam them up too much." She soothingly stroked his
back with one hand, her heart aching for his pain.

The warmth of his skin seeped through the shirting
under her palm. Her fingers found the groove of his
spine. His hard chest was against her small breasts,
and her eyes were nearly level with his tautened
mouth. She wanted to reach up and soften its harsh
outline with her own, take away the rigidly controlled
torment and bring back the wildly attractive, wonder-
fully masculine mouth that promised both firmness
and tenderness, the mouth that she loved.

She couldn't do that, but she raised a hand and tried
to smooth the suffering line from between his brows,

and stroked back his hair where it had fallen over his forehead.

And with a sense of fatalism, she knew that what she had been guarding against had crept up on her despite all her efforts. It wasn't just Benedict's mouth she loved—it was the man. Not his face or his body but everything he was—his frankly stated ambition and the secret vulnerability that drove it, the tenacity with which he pursued a goal, his unyielding pride, his stubborn will and sharp mind, his humor, his moments of generosity and tenderness. His passion, that she'd glimpsed so rarely.

It wouldn't do her any good of course, but she loved Benedict Falkner with every particle of her, body and soul, heart, and she hated Tiffany for doing this to him.

"Riley!" His hands gripped her shoulders, making her eyes widen and her heart lurch. "If I let my emotions go…" he said with peculiar intensity, and stopped there. "God, you don't know what you're asking for."

He looked angry as well as tortured now.

She looked back at him stubbornly, loosening only marginally her hold on him. She supposed he was afraid of seeming unmanly. "There's no shame in crying," she told him, "if you want to."

Something flickered across his face, as if he was torn between two emotions. "I don't want to cry," he said in a deep, uneven voice that convinced her he was lying. "I want—" Suddenly he closed his eyes, giving his head a shake as if to clear it. He still held her shoulders, but he seemed to have forgotten that.

"What?" She shifted her hands to rest them both lightly on his chest, almost unconsciously making little stroking movements. ''Let me help, Benedict. If there's anything I can do…'' Anything to hide the raging hurt that she sensed in him, that was making her hurt too.

''Anything?'' His eyes narrowed, glittering, and for an instant she felt a tiny pang of fright. His whole body had gone rigid, and she thought he wasn't even breathing. And then his hard hands pulled her forward until his mouth closed over her astonished, parted lips, and his arms wrapped about her, hard and strong and almost suffocating.

The kiss was filled with need and desperation—and desire. A dark whirlwind carrying her away, blotting out their surroundings, drowning all sound but her own wild blood humming in her ears. The world stopped, and nothing existed but her and him and their mouths, their bodies, Riley at last in Benedict's arms where she belonged—where she'd always belonged, the only place she ever wanted to be.

She never even thought of resisting. At the first touch of his mouth, she'd softened to him, her lips parting gladly, her body curving into the shape of his, her arms clinging around his neck. Her head tipped back under his kiss until her neck ached, but she didn't care.

Benedict's hands left her shoulders and one arm cradled her head, the other holding her close around her waist. He kept on kissing her, deeper and fiercer and with intense concentration, until she was dizzy with desire.

And she couldn't get enough of him. She was on tiptoe, leaning into him, giving as much as receiving, responding to passion with passion. Every nerve and fiber was alive and singing, every sense alert, aware, expectant.

When he lifted his head, she heard him say gruffly, "Oh, *God,* Riley! Are you crazy, you darling little idiot!"

"I don't see what's idiotic about offering comfort to a...friend."

"Comfort!" His eyes glinted disconcertingly. "You're very good at it, aren't you?"

"I...I hope I am." Why did he sound so bitter? It wasn't a crime, was it? Unless he thought... "What do you mean, exactly?" she enquired carefully, easing out of his slackened hold.

"I mean I'm suitably grateful," he said, "and appreciative. But I can't take advantage of your generosity this way." As she blinked up at him, puzzled and apprehensive, he added, "And under false pretences. As a matter of interest, it wasn't Tiffany who broke off our—relationship."

Not Tiffany? Her head buzzed. "I thought she was everything you ever wanted."

"She is. Everything. There's just one problem."

"What?" Riley asked. Did he still think he wasn't good enough for Tiffany? Had he given her up out of some quixotic whim? "What problem?" she reiterated, when he didn't answer.

His voice came out of the growing darkness, hard and clear and hostile.

"You."

Chapter Ten

"*Me?*" She couldn't have heard right. But she knew she had.

"I knew as soon as I'd hired you," Benedict said, "that it was the stupidest thing I'd ever done."

Riley's head lifted. "You haven't complained." Except about her wearing skimpy clothing when the lawn-mowing guy was around. "Well, hardly," she amended.

"You're too damned generous for your own good," he said, and it didn't sound complimentary. "I thought I'd made it clear your job description doesn't include sleeping with the boss."

He almost seemed to be accusing her. Riley stood up, and discovered her legs were trembling. "I know that, but…" But what? *But I love you?* She couldn't say that—it would make him feel guilty. "This had nothing to do with the job," she said, wounded. "It was a personal thing, between…between friends."

"You sleep with all your male friends, do you?" he sneered.

She gaped at him, stunned by the unwarranted implication. He was hitting out, she guessed, blindly trying to hide his own hurt by hurting someone else, and she was nearest. It wasn't fair and she wouldn't let him get away with it.

But before she could tell him so, he spoke again. "Anyway, I don't believe in mixing the personal and the professional," he said flatly. "It was a mistake, and it can't be allowed to happen again. I'll give you a month's pay in lieu of notice, but I'm terminating your employment as of now."

Riley almost choked with shocked indignation. "You're *sacking* me?"

"I prefer to call it—"

"I don't care what you *prefer* to call it!" she blazed, outraged. *"Why?"*

"Riley, try to understand—"

"Because I tried to help? Because I kissed you? Well, it wasn't my idea—you started it!" How could he do this, just because she'd overstepped the bounds of an employer/employee relationship, attempting in her no doubt clumsy and apparently wrongheaded way to assuage his obvious misery? "I was just giving you a friendly cuddle…! It's not my fault you took it as an invitation." Her conscience twinged but she ignored it. "And I don't want your month's wages, either."

"I didn't mean it that way. You've got it wrong, Riley—"

Riley was already on her way to the door. "I'll pack and be out of here in half an hour," she promised.

"Riley!"

He caught up with her in the passageway and grabbed her arm, but she shook his hand off and sprinted the rest of the way to her suite, hurtling through the saloon doors, throwing open the one to her suite. Then she yelped as Benedict blocked her from closing it, and she had to retreat from his big shadowy form when it filled the space and he thrust the door back to the wall. "Listen to me, you little wildcat!"

"Get out!" She darted toward the bedroom with some idea of closing that door in his face, although she didn't know what good it would do. There was no lock there.

Of course he followed her, grappling her to him as she turned to kick him and try to thump him with clenched fists. He hauled her against him, one hand holding her wrists, and lifted her right off the ground.

"Let me go!" She wriggled ineffectually. Her voice rose. "You promised I'd be safe here!"

"You *are* safe!" He sounded totally exasperated. "I'm not hurting you."

"I'll bite you again!" she warned.

"Just try it," Benedict said grimly. "You won't get away with that a second time." And then he turned and pushed her onto her bed underneath him, his big hard chest squashing her breasts, his thighs trapping hers. "Now keep still."

Finally she did—not so much because he was holding her down, but because the warmth and strength of him made her want to snuggle into him despite her fury, and the scent of his skin was an insidious aphrodisiac. Besides, her futile struggles were arousing him, and she needed to channel all her strength into the willpower necessary to stop herself from responding.

"I never meant this to happen," Benedict said. "But we've gone this far and you might as well know. I'm *obsessed* with you—I have been from the very first time you smiled at me after you'd just taken a chunk out of my hand."

"I didn't…" He was exaggerating again.

Benedict wasn't listening. "I told myself there was absolutely nothing about you that would turn a man on so fiercely. With those baggy clothes and no makeup you weren't even trying, but when you smiled I had this extraordinary feeling of homecoming, and then you did that thing with your tongue that you do—"

Riley gasped. "It's a habit. I have this crooked tooth."

"I know. Don't ever have it straightened. I'd just met Tiffany—"

Tiffany. Riley held her breath.

"—and everything was falling into place. I had to be crazy to even think about a big-eyed little termagant with a sharp tongue and teeth to match. But after a couple of days of you driving me to work I couldn't let you go without at least tasting that stubborn, sassy mouth."

"You kissed me," she recalled, dazedly.

"Yeah," he agreed. "Mistake number one."

Heavens, it had hardly even been a kiss. A second or two of shocking bliss for her—but she hadn't ever imagined he'd given it another thought.

"I should have *posted* you that damned receipt," he went on. "Instead I grabbed the excuse to see you again, trying to tell myself that I'd find that this stupid, inconvenient, *absurd* infatuation would have died. And there you were with Harry and that baby, and I thought…''

"I know what you thought." That she had children—Harry's child, and a son who could have been some other man's.

"I couldn't think straight. When you said you weren't with Harry after all, I just wanted to take you away from there, take you home.''

He might have said the same about a stray kitten, Riley thought resentfully.

''References never even crossed my mind until you mentioned them. You could have been a lousy housekeeper. All I knew was you could cook and, for some reason I couldn't fathom, I wanted you like hell.''

She couldn't help a thrill of erotic pride at that, at the way his voice deepened, roughened. His heart was beating against her breast, and his chest moved as he took a harsh breath. The darkness swirled about them. Again she was conscious of his physical reaction to her.

I wanted you too. But she didn't say it aloud. Somewhere in the far recesses of what was left of her mind warning bells were trying to make themselves heard.

"So I offered you Mrs. Hardy's job," Benedict went on. "Mistake number two. Here you were, living under my roof as my employee. And making it crystal clear that you weren't available.''

"I did?'' That startled her.

"I'd promised you no strings, because you were obviously suspicious. I was so scared you wouldn't take the job if I didn't swear I had no hidden motive. Nothing sexual. Then you'd hardly been here five minutes before you spelled out to me that if you were interested in a man you'd let him know it. Well, obviously you didn't want *me*. You never missed a chance to push me in Tiffany's direction.''

"You *said* you wanted her!" Riley reminded him. She squirmed again but he took no notice, except that the hard bulge against her pelvis grew even harder. She stopped abruptly.

"If I'd really wanted her I wouldn't have needed your encouragement!'' he ground out. "I *wanted* to want her, I tried to want her—she was the sort of girl I'd dreamed of marrying. I'd already decided she was the right one, and since you weren't interested and you said *she* was, besides being—''

"A better proposition,'' Riley said tartly, beginning a slow simmer as the warning bells grew louder. "Someone you could show off, someone your upwardly mobile lifestyle could use.''

"I never meant to use her,'' he growled defensively. "Dammit, I should have been able to love her. She had everything I was looking for…I thought. But you kept getting in the way. I didn't understand it but I kept thinking about you even though Tiffany was so right and you were so…different. I hoped it would wear off, that seeing you day after day would somehow shake the addiction…''

"Familiarity breeding contempt?'' Just as she had flippantly suggested to Lin that picking up after Benedict and washing his socks would cure her own futile longing for him.

"It didn't.'' His voice had flattened again. "That day I saw Kevin ogling you, and you laughing with him, flirting, I was blind with jealousy.''

"I wasn't flirting!''

He ignored her. "When I kissed you and you kissed me back I thought maybe you felt something too. But then you flew at me, and I was terrified you'd leave, so I groveled—"

"I don't recall you doing any groveling." She scowled.

"Apologized, then. I would have groveled if necessary. All I could think of was not letting you go. And then Harry spent the night with you—"

Riley gaped. "Well, yes he did, but—"

"I saw you from the summerhouse, on your bed with him, practically naked."

"I wasn't…"

"Well, he was. And I don't suppose it took you long. I heard him snoring next morning in your sitting room. I suppose it was more comfortable for two."

What? Riley's head swam. "You are *nuts!*" she spat at him, furious with him for jumping to conclusions, listening at keyholes when he could have just *asked* her, if he wanted to know what was going on. She began to struggle again. "Get off me! Get…off!"

She heaved at him, but her efforts would have had no effect if he hadn't chosen that moment to release her wrists and reach out to switch on the bedside light.

As it was she unbalanced him, and he fell off the bed to the floor, twisting to land on his back and break her fall as she tumbled on top of him.

Riley took the chance to wrench herself away and stand up, and Benedict quickly followed. The light made her blink. "I don't have to make excuses to you!" she said loudly, her fists clenched. Where Harry had slept or who he'd slept with was actually none of his business. But she'd tell him all the same.

Benedict said, "I'm not asking you to."

"I did offer Harry the bed in my room but—"

He just bulldozed over her attempt at explanation, his raised voice battering hers down. "I don't even *care* who you've slept with, but I hope you haven't taken the same chances with Harry—or anyone else— that you seemed willing to take with me. Do you know how many women he's been with?"

A hot, bright light dawned behind her eyes. He thought she was promiscuous, that she'd have sex with *anyone*. He'd been saying so all evening in different ways. He didn't want to hear what she had to say, and she was sick to death of it.

Between gritted teeth, she said, "I've no idea. I forgot to count the notches on his bedpost last time I was there!"

The sudden whiteness in his cheeks should have been a satisfaction to her. Instead she felt sick and ashamed of herself. "I didn't mean—"

Benedict overrode her retraction, advancing on her with such a threatening expression that she squealed breathlessly and retreated. "You're not married to him yet," he said belligerently, making Riley mentally reel. "And you won't be—as long as I'm around to stop you."

Marry Harry? When had she ever suggested such a thing? And where did Benedict Falkner get off telling her who she should or shouldn't marry anyway? "I'll marry whoever I damn well please!" she informed him haughtily. "And what the hell do you think gives *you* the right to stop me?"

"Do you fancy bigamy?"

He *was* mad. Completely round the twist, out of his tree. She should be calling the men in white coats. *"Bigamy?"*

"I kept telling myself you were the wrong one, until I watched you on that swing and it finally hit me that you were the *only* one—right or wrong, it made no difference. But Harry got in first."

"Benedict—"

"It was my own fault—I should have faced reality ages ago. I thought I could love Tiffany. Any man should be able to love Tiffany. I'm quite fond of her. When I finally resigned myself to the fact that I had no real wish to take her to bed, it was too late."

"Too late?" What was he talking about now?

"You were happy, and I realized I had no right to tear you away from Harry if he was what you wanted."

Finding her voice, she said, "You've no need to—"

"But then you 'comforted' me." He *still* wasn't listening. "And I'm telling you, Riley, you've done it now. You can't expect a man who's been given a glimpse of heaven to tamely return to earth—not without a fight." He grabbed her shoulders as if he wanted to shake her. "You won't be marrying anyone else because you're bloody well going to marry me!"

Riley hadn't fought her way through a childhood with brothers galore for nothing. Even the older ones had learned that telling her what to do was worse than waving a red rag at a tetchy bull. Especially when the person doing the telling was a male.

She gave him an almighty shove, adrenaline lending her strength enough to free herself and even set him back a step or two. Her eyes felt red-hot, and her cheeks were burning too. Her voice rose to fishwife level. "I wouldn't marry you if you were the last...*creature* on earth!'' she told him. "You arrogant, self-satisfied, patronizing jerk!''

Then she told him a lot more about himself, none of it accurate, most of it extremely unlikely, and all of it slanderous. And a lot of it with the potential to land her in jail if uttered in public.

Benedict listened, at first with a bleak expression, then scowling, the scowl gradually giving way to a grin of awed admiration. Finally, to Riley's total chagrin, he folded his arms and leaned on the nearest wall, unmistakably enjoying himself.

When she'd run out of steam and her voice had started cracking, he straightened and said, "Does that mean no?''

No to *what?* He hadn't even *asked* her to marry him—just informed her that she was going to. Dangerously close to tears, Riley stamped her foot on the carpet in frustration and wailed, "Oh, *go away!*''

He looked a little startled, then came toward her and gave her a quick hug and dropped a kiss on the top of her head. "Okay," he soothed. "I guess you need some time to get used to the idea.''

He left her staring blankly at the door as he closed it gently behind him. Finally she dredged up a tattered remnant of defiance and yelled through the panels, "I *told* you, not if you were my last hope!''

She thought she heard a faint sound of laughter before the outer door closed, and she collapsed on the bed in a flood of overwrought, mortifying tears.

An hour later Lin opened the door of the flat to her. "You've been crying!'' she said with horror and immediately hugged her close. "What's happened,

Riley?" she asked anxiously. "You didn't say on the phone…"

That was another reason to not ever allow herself to be driven to tears—her eyes would be bloodshot and her lids swollen for hours yet. "I've left my job," she said. "Thanks for letting me stay, Lin."

"Did that man do something to you?" Lin asked darkly.

"Nothing I didn't want him to do. Nothing I haven't been wanting him to do ever since I laid eyes on him. I'd rather not talk about it, okay? And I don't want the others to see me tonight."

Lin's sloe eyes momentarily rounded. But she said promptly, "Sure. Come on, I've made up a bed in my room."

Riley fell exhausted onto the mattress and, contrary to all her expectations, slept like a log.

She was awakened by birdsong outside the window—or perhaps the voices in the hall. Lin's light voice, the words indistinguishable, and a deep, penetrating male one saying loudly, "Then I'll just wait here until she's awake."

Benedict. Riley sat up abruptly. Benedict was out there, bullying poor Lin.

Swearing under her breath, she crawled from the sleeping bag, scrabbled in the overnighter she'd hastily packed, found her satin wrap and dragged it out, crumpled but decent. Throwing it on, she viciously tightened the belt. Lin was still agitatedly talking, but maybe Benedict had decided to ignore her, because he wasn't replying.

Riley couldn't find a comb. Even Lin's dressing table top yielded no such thing. Pushing her hands through her hair, she sighed, and stumbled to the door, blinking herself awake.

Lin turned a worried face to her. "Riley, Mr. Falkner wants to talk to you."

Benedict was leaning against the closed front door, feet apart and arms folded, looking like a security guard. No, looking like Benedict, she thought forlornly. Handsome and determined and heart-turningly desirable.

"What do you want?" she demanded, pushing at her sleep-disheveled hair again. Her tongue crept to her tooth and she sternly halted it, remembering what he'd said about that. She pushed her chin forward instead.

"To talk to you," he confirmed.

Riley said scornfully, "You talked to me last night."

"Yes, too much."

So had he come to tell her he hadn't meant any of it? Her head lifted, her chin becoming even more pugnacious.

Benedict started toward her, a purposeful look on his face, and Lin hopped out of his way with a small squeak.

Riley looked around wildly and screeched, in a voice that would have roused a whole mortuary, *"Ha-rry!"*

Harry's door was flung open, and he blundered into the wide passageway. "Wha—?" Sooty stubble covered his cheeks and chin. He wore only black satin boxer shorts patterned all over with lipstick imprints. Peering at the morning light with bleary eyes, he raked a hand through his hair until it stood on end, then shook his head and rubbed at his eyelids.

In the mornings Harry was, if anything, more nearly comatose than Riley. She was mildly surprised he'd even heard her cry for help.

Benedict stopped dead as Harry almost blundered into him.

Harry turned to the two women. "Whazzamatter?"

"We have an intruder," Riley said briskly. "Throw him out, will you?"

Benedict said in long-suffering tones, "Riley—"

"Go *on*, Harry," she urged. "Get rid of him."

Harry was a good head taller than Benedict, and his weightlifting had developed an impressive amount of muscle. The mere threat should have been enough to send Benedict scuttling.

But Benedict stood his ground.

"Um, how about you go, mate?" Harry coaxed hopefully.

"Sorry." Benedict looked firm and unafraid. "I should tell you," he added almost apologetically, "I've got a black belt in judo and a couple of cups for middleweight boxing. And I won't go until I've had a word with Riley."

Harry looked him up and down carefully and scratched at the stubble on his chin. His eyes slid anxiously to Riley. "I've got that audition in L.A. next week," he mumbled. "Don't wanna get my face messed up, Ri. Why don't you talk to the guy? He won't hurt you, will he?" Turning to Benedict, he flexed his shoulders and tried to look intimidating. "You won't hurt her?"

"I won't lay a finger on her," Benedict promised, gazing at the other man speculatively. "Unless she asks me to."

Riley snorted at that, but he ignored her. Lin

hopped from one foot to the other and gave another muffled little squeak. Harry finger-combed his hair again, yawned, and muttered, "Yeah, well, I guess I better have a shower now I'm up."

Fuming, Riley watched her protector amble off to the bathroom. Benedict was already at her side, hands ostentatiously shoved into his pockets. "Where can we be private?"

"The sitting room, I suppose," she conceded.

Lin said bravely, "I'll come with you if you like, Riley."

"Thanks, Lin." Riley gave her a grateful smile. "But it's okay." Casting a fulminating glance at Benedict, she added, "I'll get rid of him soon."

"Never…" she thought she heard him say as she led the way to the sitting room. A tiny shiver of excitement ran down her spine, dismaying her.

He followed her into the room and shut the door. As she swung round, he said, "Don't worry. If you scream again I'm sure your little friend will ring the police. Why did you lie to me?"

"Lie?"

"You're no more going to marry that pretty boy out there than you would the man in the moon."

"Harry's not a pretty boy, and I never said I was going to marry him," Riley pointed out irritably. "I said he wants to get married—to Aneta."

"Who the hell's Aneta?"

"Rosalita's mother. You met her when she came to pick up Rosalita, remember?"

He scowled. "I thought she was going to marry that American guy who was with her."

"Right now she doesn't want to marry anyone. I know exactly how she feels!"

"I got it all wrong yesterday," he said.

"You sure did."

"Well, what was I supposed to think? Even Tiffany thought you and Harry were…were—"

"Sleeping together?" How on earth would Tiffany have got that idea? "What would she know?"

"You were jealous."

Riley bristled. "Who says?"

"Tiffany, of course. The night Harry came and stayed, you were quite sharp about her talking to him, she told me. She thought it was funny."

"I was busy—a bit frazzled, I expect." A barefaced lie. She'd been defending, as she thought, Benedict's territory. Tiffany had just put a wrong interpretation on her reaction.

Emulating him, she pushed her hands into the pockets of her robe, because they were shaking and she didn't want him to see. "How…how did Tiffany take it when you dumped her?"

Impatient, he said, "We're still friends. And I didn't dump her."

"I suppose you told her you hoped you would be?" she asked scornfully. "And what else would you call it?"

"*She* said she'd like to be friends. I agreed."

"The poor girl—hiding her broken heart!"

"She doesn't *have* a broken heart! And I didn't come here to talk about Tiffany!"

"We have to talk about her!"

"For God's sake why?"

"Because you let me…and her…think you loved her."

"I never told her that. And I didn't tell you that, either. You shouldn't jump to conclusions."

"You said she wasn't your girlfriend, *yet.*"

"I hardly knew you when I said that. I hardly knew *her!*"

"You told me you focus on a goal and stick to it. And you certainly gave me the impression she was the one you were focused on."

He lifted a shoulder. "*You* kept telling me how right she was, that she was everything I wanted. Everyone seemed to think so. On that boat trip with her parents her father hinted that he'd approve. I should have been happy to know that, but instead I felt guilty, because I wasn't in love with Tiffany, and it finally dawned on me that I never would be. The weekend was a bit of a strain. Then I came home to you, and…I realized what a fool I'd been. Only I was afraid I'd led Tiffany up the garden path. I had to sort things out with her first, before I could tell you how I felt."

"You meant to break it off with her?"

"It was easier than I'd expected…or deserved. When I said we had to talk seriously, she started going on about how she'd planned not to marry too young, and how she really liked me *but…*"

"Maybe she was pretending."

"No," he concluded positively. "I hadn't even begun to explain. Like I said, we parted the best of friends. That's all there is to it, Riley. *Now* can we talk about us?"

"Us?" Riley said warily.

"You and me…getting married?"

"I told you last night—"

"That you wouldn't marry me if I were your last hope."

She ought to repeat it. But she didn't quite dare to

shut the door on a glimmer of hope...of glory. Still, she wasn't going to let him walk all over her. "You didn't ask me—"

"I know. When the chips are down and I'm backed into a corner I tend to take the gloves off and go for raw force." He grimaced. "A legacy of my past. It often works in business, but this isn't business. This is my life. I'm trying to be civilized about it, though my instinct is to toss you over my shoulder and haul you off to the cave." He paused, and when he spoke she could tell he was making an effort to sound humble. "Will you marry me, Riley?"

Time seemed to hold its breath. The bird was still singing outside, and Riley realized it was only minutes since she'd woken to hear Benedict saying he'd wait for her.

But for how long?

She was tempted—oh, so tempted. Only it wouldn't do. It would never do. "No."

She turned away from him, her arms folded across her chest, hiding her breaking heart, holding it together.

The silence went on for so long, she thought maybe he'd silently left. Then she heard him take a rasping breath. "Do you mind telling me why?"

Riley could almost have laughed at that, except she was afraid it would turn into a sob. Her hands curling into fists, she made her voice hard. "Guess."

"You don't love me?"

Riley lifted one shoulder in a shrug. That was one lie she couldn't bring herself to utter. Why didn't he just go away? Wasn't that what a man—a gentleman—was supposed to do when his proposal was declined?

Only she knew that, despite his carefully cultivated veneer of sophistication, Benedict wasn't a gentleman. Never had been, and underneath probably never would be. All man, yes. Gentle, yes—when he needed to be. But let a woman off the hook just because she was female and he was male? No.

"Look at me, Riley," he said. "Look at me and tell me you're not one bit in love with me. If you can."

The arrogance of the man. She whipped up a spurious anger to shield herself before she faced him again, defiantly. "I'm not...I don't..."

He didn't look arrogant. He looked taut and square-shouldered, as if tensed for a blow. And his expression was rigidly neutral, but in his eyes something glowed, deep and steady—something dangerously close to affection.

Damn the man! "Well, what do you expect?" she cried wildly. "You don't really love me!"

His brows shot up. "Last night—"

"You said I was an obsession—told me I was a *nothing,* that you couldn't understand why you were attracted to me. I ruined your plans to marry the perfect woman to go with your perfect home and your perfect business and your perfect lifestyle and give you one point two perfect children. I'm the opposite of everything you've worked so hard for. You want the princess in the tower, you've fought for years to win the right to have her, and I'm just a-an ordinary woman! *And* you practically called me a slut!" she recalled. "I *don't* sleep around with my friends and I'm not anyone's for the asking, especially not yours! Not that my sex life or lack of it is any of your business!"

"Hell!" he said, light dawning in his face. "I really messed up, didn't I? Riley, you're *not* a nothing! You *never* could be a *nothing*. You're vibrant and gutsy and capable and compassionate and strong. Besides being cute and sweet and sassy, and you fit in my arms like you belong there. And I never said you were a slut. I said I don't care how many men you've slept with. As long as I'm the last one—the only one. Because you're the only woman I'll ever want."

Riley clung to her anger for seconds, but how could she maintain it when he was looking so sincere and so anxious and so...darling. "Really?" She was full of doubt and suspicion, warring with the obstinate ray of hope.

"I was so blinkered by my narrow-minded one-eyed goals I didn't recognize what was right in front of me. Like someone fossicking for gold who finds a diamond and throws it away because he's too stupid to see what it is."

There was a rap on the door. "Riley?" Lin called. "Are you all right?"

Riley, caught up in the extraordinary things Benedict was saying, took a moment to respond, unable to tear her gaze from him. "Yes, fine."

Maybe, just maybe, she was going to be, after all.

"Harry's here," Lin said through the panels. "And Logie."

Benedict's face broke into an unholy grin. "Harry's there," he said softly. "All ready to defend you—as long as he doesn't mar his looks."

"He would if it was really necessary," Riley retorted, shaking herself back to normality.

"You know it isn't," Benedict said.

She went past him and opened the door. Lin was

hovering there, Harry trying not to look apprehensive just behind her, and Logie with his elbows sticking out, like an aggressive grasshopper. "It's okay," she said. "Thanks, but I don't need anyone."

Lin looked relieved. "Okay, boys." She dismissed them with a wave of her hand. "Sorry to interrupt," she added to Riley.

Riley closed the door, rounding on Benedict. "Are you trying to say you love me?"

"*Of course I love you!* What else have I been saying for the past twenty minutes? What did you think I was trying to say last night?"

"That I've messed up your well-planned life," she said frankly. "That you resent me like mad because you can't stop wanting me. Very…flattering," she added snarkily. And almost unbelievable. "But no basis for marriage."

Benedict groaned, and took a hand out of his pocket to hit his forehead. "I was mad, and muddled. I didn't mean any of it. You know, when you said just now that I wanted a perfect wife to go with my perfect home and my perfect lifestyle…?"

Riley nodded warily.

"Well, I got this really claustrophobic feeling. It sounded so…boring, so predictable. And I thought, life with Riley would never be like that. Life with Riley would be stimulating and funny and…wild and wonderful and loving. And *real*. Nothing like the artificial life I've built, that I thought was so important. I can't imagine living without you anymore. After that weekend with Tiffany's family, when I walked in on you in my room, I was so glad to see you—"

"You looked happy," she remembered.

"You make me happy," he said simply. "Just by

being near me. I wanted to pick you up right then and kiss you senseless, just because you were there in my home. And last night I couldn't sleep because you weren't.''

Riley bit her lip, feeling stupidly guilty.

"You might taunt me and tease me and go off like a firecracker when I make you mad, but you'll never bore me," he told her. "I can count on that."

"What if I embarrass you?" she asked him, still doubting. "I don't know much about clothes."

"You can learn if you want to. But if fashion doesn't interest you, don't bother."

"I won't always say the right thing, behave the right way, like Tiffany."

"Do you think I do? That anybody does? You care about people, and that's the essence of saying the right thing, behaving the right way. Everything else is unimportant. And anyone who embarrasses *you* will have me to contend with."

"With your black belt and your boxing titles. I've never seen any cups in the house. Didn't you keep them?"

"I've never boxed."

"Judo?"

"A bit. No black belt."

"You lied!" She tried to sound shocked.

"I was desperate. Riley...I've been a fool all my life, one way or another. I know now that money isn't what matters. Position doesn't matter. Status symbols aren't what life is about. Love is. You can't force it and you don't choose it, but when it comes, it's the most precious thing in the world. And it's worth giving up everything else for. Everything that I thought was important and necessary. It's all dross if I don't have you.''

Another knock on the door. ''Riley? Sam and Logie have left. Okay if we go now? Harry's giving me a lift.''

''Go ahead,'' she called. ''Thanks for the bed, Lin. I'll lock up.''

Seconds later the front door banged. An engine started outside.

''We're alone?'' Benedict asked.

''Seems so.''

''Am I right,'' he said, ''in thinking you're having second thoughts about turning me down?''

Riley regarded him thoughtfully. ''Could be.''

He took his other hand out of his pocket. ''I could try persuasion, only I promised I wouldn't touch you unless you asked.''

''What sort of persuasion?'' she said softly.

''If you want to find out...you know what you have to do.''

It was torture. She wanted him so much, could feel him wanting her. The wanting shimmered in the air between them, tangible, breathtaking. Riley swallowed. ''Touch me,'' she whispered.

His eyes gleamed, but for seconds longer he tormented her. Then he reached for her. ''Come here.'' And he lifted her and sank down on the old lumpy sofa, cradling her on his knee. ''Where?'' he demanded.

Riley's fist thumped his shoulder. ''You know where! Everywhere.'' And she kissed him.

Instantly it was unclear who was kissing whom. Her hands were in his hair, his hands slipping on the satin of her wrap.

The sofa was small and they ended up on the floor, their limbs entangled, mouths locked. He grabbed a cushion for her head before he kissed her again and she wound her arms about his neck.

Benedict turned onto his back, lifting her over him, stroking her from shoulder to thigh, and she opened her mouth against his neck.

"Bite me now," he said, and against a shudder of primitive response she left her mark on his skin. He returned the compliment, but oh, so gently, his teeth grazing her shoulder as he pushed away the robe. She shivered all over with delicious sensation. But when his fingers intruded further she caught his hand in hers and said, "I think we're shocking Homer."

She would show him she wasn't, as she'd accused him of thinking, just anyone's for the asking. She loved him to distraction but he deserved a little punishment.

Benedict looked up at the battered plaster gnome. "He looks to me as if he's seen a thing or two before." But he took the hint and eased away a little, adjusting their positions so they were side by side.

"Mmm," Riley murmured against his chest, where her cheek was resting. "Mr. Falkner, does this mean I can call you Ben?"

"You can call me whatever you like. One of these days," he said, "we'll have to find a bed."

"When we're married," she answered.

There was a tense silence. "Riley?" He tugged at her hair, making her look at him. Echoing her words, he said, "Does this mean yes?"

"Mmm, maybe," Riley teased. "I might need a bit more...persuasion?" she suggested wistfully. "You're so awfully good at it."

He gave her a severe look. "Listen, you little—"

"Slut?"

"Baggage. Is it yes or no?"

"Ooh...raw force?" Her eyes widened.

"Riley..." he warned.

"Yes," she said hastily. "But it's such fun being persuaded."

Benedict turned over until she was underneath him, and kissed her deeply. "Thank you," he said huskily, raising his head at last. "Maybe I could persuade you to have my baby sometime?"

Riley's finger traced his mouth. "Sometime," she agreed. "But that might take an *awful* lot of persuasion."

Benedict lazily reached out and pulled the Santa stocking down over Homer's wide, painted eyes.

"No problem," he promised, his mouth lowering again to Riley's, the final words lost against her lips. "No problem at all."

*   *   *   *   *

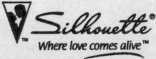

presents rising star

MYRNA MACKENZIE's

romantic miniseries

Where the highest bidder wins...love!

Ethan Bennington begins the bidding
in **August 2002** with
BOUGHT BY THE BILLIONAIRE (SR#1610)

Join Dylan Valentine in **October 2002**
when he discovers
THE BILLIONAIRE'S BARGAIN (SR#1622)

And watch for the conclusion to this trilogy
in **December 2002** with Spencer Fairfield, as
THE BILLIONAIRE BORROWS A BRIDE (SR#1634)

Available at your favorite retail outlet

Where love comes alive™

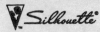

SPECIAL EDITION™

Was it something in the water...
or something in the air?

Because bachelors in Bridgewater, Texas,
are becoming a vanishing breed—fast!

**Don't miss these three exciting stories of Texas
cowboys by favorite author Jodi O'Donnell:**

Deke Larrabie returns to discover
someone *else* he left behind....

THE COME-BACK COWBOY
(Special Edition #1494)
September 2002

Connor Brody meets his match and gives her

THE RANCHER'S PROMISE
(Silhouette Romance #1619)
October 2002

Griff Corbin learns about true
friendship and love when he falls for

HIS BEST FRIEND'S BRIDE
(Silhouette Romance #1625)
November 2002

Available at your favorite retail outlet.

Where love comes alive™

SSEBRB

SILHOUETTE *Romance*™

**Lost siblings, secret worlds,
tender seduction—live the fantasy in...**

A TALE OF THE SEA

**Separated and hidden since childhood,
Phoebe, Kai, Saegar and Thalassa
must reunite in order to safeguard
their underwater kingdom.
But who will protect *them*...?**

July 2002
MORE THAN MEETS THE EYE
by Carla Cassidy (SR #1602)

August 2002
IN DEEP WATERS
by Melissa McClone (SR #1608)

September 2002
CAUGHT BY SURPRISE
by Sandra Paul (SR #1614)

October 2002
FOR THE TAKING
by Lilian Darcy (SR #1620)

***Look for these titles wherever
Silhouette books are sold!***

Silhouette®
Where love comes alive™

buy books

Your one-stop shop for great reads at great prices. We have all your favorite Harlequin, Silhouette, MIRA and Steeple Hill books, as well as a host of other bestsellers in Other Romances. Discover a wide array of new releases, bargains and hard-to-find books today!

learn to write

Become the writer you always knew you could be: get tips and tools on how to craft the perfect romance novel and have your work critiqued by professional experts in romance fiction. Follow your dream now!

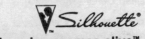

Where love comes alive™—online...

Visit us at
www.eHarlequin.com

If you enjoyed what you just read,
then we've got an offer you can't resist!

Take 2 bestselling love stories FREE!

Plus get a FREE surprise gift!

SILHOUETTE *Romance*

COMING NEXT MONTH

#1618 THE WILL TO LOVE—Lindsay McKenna
Morgan's Mercenaries: Ultimate Rescue
With her community destroyed by an earthquake, Deputy Sheriff
Kerry Chelton turned to Sergeant Quinn Grayson to help establish order
and rebuild. But when Kerry was injured, Quinn began to realize that no
devastation compared to losing Kerry....

#1619 THE RANCHER'S PROMISE—Jodi O'Donnell
Bridgewater Bachelors
Lara Dearborn's new boss was none other than Connor Brody—the
son of her sworn enemy! Connor had worked his entire life to escape
Mick Brody's legacy. But could he have a future with Lara when the
truth about their fathers came out?

#1620 FOR THE TAKING—Lilian Darcy
A Tale of the Sea
Thalassa Morgan wanted to put the past behind her, something that Lou-
can—claimant of the Pacifica throne—wouldn't allow. Reluctantly she
returned to Pacifica as his wife to restore order to their kingdom. But
her sexy, uncompromising husband proved to be far more dangerous
than the nightmares haunting her....

#1621 CROWNS AND A CRADLE—Valerie Parv
The Carramer Legacy
She thought she'd won a vacation to Carramer—but discovered her
true identity! Sarah McInnes's grandfather was Prince Henry Valmont—
and her one-year-old son the royal heir! Now, handsome, intense Prince
Josquin had to persuade her to stay—but were his motives political or
personal?

#1622 THE BILLIONAIRE'S BARGAIN—Myrna Mackenzie
The Wedding Auction
What does a confirmed bachelor stuck caring for his eighteen-month-
old twin brothers do? Buy help from a woman auctioning her services
for charity! But beautiful April Pruitt was no ordinary nanny, and
Dylan Valentine wondered if his bachelorhood was the next item on
the block!

#1623 THE SHERIFF'S 6-YEAR-OLD SECRET—Donna Clayton
The Thunder Clan
Nathan Thunder avoided intimate relationships—and discovering he had
an independent six-year-old daughter wasn't going to change that!
Gwen Fleming wanted to help her teenage brother. Could two mis-
matched families find true love?